"I'm afraid I love you, Gideon," Maggie said.

He stopped moving and stared down at her. "We met yesterday."

"That doesn't matter. If it was just passion, there wouldn't be a problem, because that's a fleeting thing. When it was over, you'd go back to San Francisco and I'd go to Richmond and that'd be it. But love is different, so I thought I'd better warn you."

"Warn me?"

Maggie's smile was rueful. "My family's a bit unusual, Gideon, and one of the ways is that it seems to be stamped in our cells to fall in love only once . . . and with the right person."

Holding her in his arms, Gideon stared down at her. "What are you saying, Maggie?"

"That once we become lovers, you're mine. You'll belong to me in the same way that I'll belong to you. In my world, Gideon, love is forever."

After a moment, he spoke. "And if I only wanted an affair?"

"It wouldn't matter." Her voice was serene. "You could leave me once it was over, walk away and never look back. I wouldn't chase after you. But you'd still be mine. And you'd always know it. Real love brands you inside and out. Whether you feel it or someone feels it for you, you're still branded. . . ."

WHAT ARE *LOVESWEPT* ROMANCES?

They are stories of true romance and touching emotion. We believe those two very important ingredients are constants in our highly sensual and very believable stories in the *LOVESWEPT* line. Our goal is to give you, the reader, stories of consistently high quality that may sometimes make you laugh, sometimes make you cry, but are always fresh and creative and contain many delightful surprises within their pages.

Most romance fans read an enormous number of books. Those they truly love, they keep. Others may be traded with friends and soon forgotten. We hope that each *LOVESWEPT* romance will be a treasure—a "keeper." We will always try to publish

*LOVE STORIES YOU'LL NEVER FORGET
BY AUTHORS YOU'LL ALWAYS REMEMBER*

The Editors

LOVESWEPT® • 408

Kay Hooper
Once Upon A Time: Through the Looking Glass

BANTAM BOOKS
NEW YORK • TORONTO • LONDON • SYDNEY • AUCKLAND

THROUGH THE LOOKING GLASS

A Bantam Book / July 1990

*If you would be interested in receiving protective vinyl
covers for your Loveswept books, please write to this address
for information:*

Loveswept
Bantam Books
P.O. Box 985
Hicksville, NY 11802

ISBN 0-553-44038-1

Published simultaneously in the United States and Canada

PRINTED IN THE UNITED STATES OF AMERICA

OPM   0 9 8 7 6 5 4 3 2 1

Author's Note

Alice discovered a strange new world when she stepped through her looking glass. Not always a safe world, it held nonsense and lunacy, danger and charm.

But that was only a story. What would a man find if he stepped through a looking glass? A Mad Hatter's tea party? Or something even more unexpected?

Prologue

"Am I disturbing you, child?" The lovely feminine voice that issued from the telephone receiver held an abstracted tone, but it couldn't obscure the more resonant notes of a strong and forceful personality. Her voice had a mysterious quality that Maggie had never been able to put her finger on.

"No, Aunt Julia. I'm alone." Aunt Julia never wanted to intrude on Maggie's personal life and never asked probing questions, but seemed to take it for granted that her infrequent calls probably interrupted athletic bouts of youthful sex. Especially since she tended to call very late at night.

Maggie pushed herself up on an elbow and rubbed her eyes blearily before peering at her bedside clock. Par for the course: It was two A.M.

"Alone? At your age? Really, Maggie, you—well, never mind. It's your own business, certainly, and with all the risks you young people have to contend with these days, I suppose you're wise to be selective."

Politely, Maggie said, "That is true. I just wish you'd get it through your head that I don't have a line of hopeful lovers waiting outside my door. I told you when I was ten that I was going to wait for Mr. Right, and I haven't changed my mind. Silly of me to be an idealist, I realize, but there it is."

"You haven't found him yet I take it?"

"Hardly. There are a number of misters running around out there, but not one of them has been right for me. Did you call to check on the progress of my love life?"

"You know better. I'd never intrude."

Maggie laughed softly. "Sure. You also never mind the time zones. It's two A.M. here, Aunt Julia."

"I'm sorry, child. But I'm afraid I have bad news."

Sitting up in bed, Maggie said, "Not Uncle Cyrus?"

"Oh, no. It's your cousin Merlin."

Maggie remembered this particular cousin, though it had been years since she'd seen him. That was generally the case with her relatives. A large family and long-lived, they were spread out over the globe and rarely got together for clan gatherings. Which was, Maggie had privately decided, all to the good. To say that most of her relatives were peculiar was to understate the matter. They ranged from mildly eccentric to certifiably mad—though none was, to her knowledge, dangerous.

The undisputed heads of the clan were Aunt Julia and Uncle Cyrus, and both were . . . unusual. Definitely unusual. The younger generations of the family called them aunt and uncle, but the actual relationships were vague. Maggie didn't know their ages or, really, anything else concrete about them, and when in a mad moment she'd tried to research her family tree, she'd backtracked as far as the turn of the century before losing her nerve. By that point, the tree branches had been weighted down with so many colorful characters and peculiar stories that she decided she didn't want to know how it all began.

Merlin was indeed her cousin, though she wasn't sure how far removed. His name was legitimate, the gift of a romantic-minded mother, and he'd naturally ended up in a carnival. He'd done the most marvelous magic act years back; Maggie thought she must have been six when she'd first seen it. He had seemed old then.

"How old is Merlin?" she suddenly asked.

"I don't think that matters now, child, because he's dead," Aunt Julia replied frankly.

"Oh. I'm sorry. When's the wake?" Her clan wasn't noticeably Irish, they simply liked parties, and without exception every one of them hated wearing black.

"Day after tomorrow. Of course you'll come."

"Of course. Where?" The last family wake had been held in New Orleans. There had been marching, Maggie remembered. And trumpets.

Aunt Julia sighed and for the first time sounded a bit irritated. "He wanted his ashes scattered over Disneyland, but the authorities wouldn't hear of it. Cyrus tried, but he just couldn't bring them around. We've had to settle for Niagara Falls. Not as good, but he did say many times that he wanted to go over it in a barrel."

Maggie accepted that without a blink. "Almost as good, then. I'll arrange to be there. How did he die?"

"The police ruled it accidental, Maggie, but that's

ridiculous. He was murdered." Aunt Julia stated her opinion just the way one standing in the midst of a cloudburst would state that it was raining. Absolute authority. There was no point arguing with her; only Uncle Cyrus had ever been known to succeed in getting her to back away from such an unequivocally stated opinion.

"Really?" Maggie asked. "Members of our family don't generally get bumped off." Her peculiar family *did* have a rather impressive record of good health and few enemies.

"We don't have stupid accidents either. You've just begun your summer vacation, haven't you? After the wake, perhaps you could find Wonderland and look around a bit? We should know the truth, child. For our own peace of mind. And for poor Merlin, of course. He'll hate it if he can never leave the area of that wretched well he was pushed into."

Maggie followed that reasoning only because she vaguely recalled that Cousin Merlin had believed strongly in ghosts and in the conviction that an unresolved or violent death chained a helpless spirit to the spot of his or her untimely demise. She wasn't particularly surprised by her aunt's request; over the past ten years, Maggie had become something of a troubleshooter on family problems. Apparently, a possibly murdered cousin fell into that category.

"All right, Aunt Julia. You can fill me in when I get there. I'll get a flight tomorrow if I can."

"Wonderful, child. We'll see you then."

Julia hung up the phone and sat gazing somewhat thoughtfully across the big old desk. "This time, you've surprised me, Cyrus," she said. "To send that delicate child into such a potentially dangerous situation alone—"

He chuckled softly. "Delicate? In appearance, certainly, but Maggie is no frail flower, sweet. She has an astonishingly good mind—particularly considering her upbringing. Of all our descendants she has inherited the highest degree of tolerance, the best-developed sense of the absurd, and the most childlike spirit. Combined with her sheer intelligence, those traits make her a rather formidable young woman. I'm not at all surprised she has yet to find a man to match her."

"And so?" Julia prompted.

"I've found one for her," Cyrus finished simply.

"You'll send him to Wonderland?"

Cyrus's vivid dark eyes shone with the radiant intelligence that only Julia saw unshuttered. "Like Alice, he must fall down the rabbit hole. If he is to see Maggie clearly, he must see all that she is."

After a moment Julia smiled faintly. "Daunting for him, poor man."

"He will survive." Cyrus chuckled again richly. "He may even prevail."

"Will we help?"

"Perhaps. We will certainly be ready to do so. At the very least we'll keep a close watch, as usual."

Julia nodded and smiled wryly. "I suppose you know what you're doing."

"Always, my sweet. Always."

It didn't strike Maggie as at all peculiar to find that the owner of the Wonderland carnival bore the improbable name of Balthasar Bundy; she knew of odder names, principally among her own family.

Her own given name had been strictly confined to her birth certificate, since she refused to use it; her understanding father had suggested "Maggie" as a reasonable compromise on her fifth birthday.

It didn't strike her as strange either that Balthasar instantly welcomed her into his troupe of carnies; she'd taken care both to dress and act suitably, after all, and her claims as an animal trainer would have been proven valid if he'd given her a chance to demonstrate.

What struck her as somewhat bizarre was Balthasar's immediate and cheerful request that she "mind the store" while he journeyed off to Africa in search of a rhinoceros.

"But why me?" she asked curiously as he bustled about his rather exotic caravan throwing colorful clothing into a battered suitcase. She had silently debated and discarded a question about the realistic possibilities of not only locating and capturing a rhinoceros, but then sneaking it off African soil and onto American soil in violation of a number of laws. To her experienced gaze, he bore all the signs of a man who would consider such a question totally pointless.

Balthasar gave her a comical look of surprise. "Well, my dear, no one else here could do it."

Maggie had too much experience with amiable lunatics to question this one further. And since she had several good reasons to believe he'd had nothing to do with Cousin Merlin's unfortunate "accident," she didn't try to prevent him from leaving. She merely asked a half dozen or so sensible questions and stood pointedly in his way until he answered them, then accepted the key to the money box—which was currently housed in the floor of the boa constrictor's cage—and promised to make herself at home in his caravan until he returned.

Then she waved good-bye from the doorway of said caravan as he rode off into the sunset in a battered 1958 black Caddie.

A muffled thump behind her made her jump. She turned to stare at the bed. It had come down from the wall, which it was supposed to do only after being unfastened. Balthasar had warned her in passing that the catch was defective. She gazed at the plush red velvet spread and gold-tasseled pillows, then allowed her pained eyes to take in the remainder of the caravan. Not that there was a great deal of space left once the bed came down.

There was a worn path in the faded carpet around the foot of the bed, which indicated that Balthasar habitually made certain he wasn't walking under the bed when it decided to drop. There was an emerald velvet love seat wedged in near the door with a scarred wooden table and oil lamp beside it. There was a wardrobe, which Balthasar had emptied, leaning a bit drunkenly on two shortened legs beside the narrow trapdoor that allowed access to the driver's seat of the wagon. And taking up the remaining floor space was a gleaming old rolltop desk, its every pigeonhole stuffed beyond capacity with yellowed papers.

Maggie heard herself sigh, which wasn't exactly surprising. She turned again and looked out on what was, she thought, a cross between a gypsy camp, a moth-eaten circus, and a lunatic asylum on wheels.

"Interesting place to spend a vacation," she murmured, and ventured forth to meet the inmates.

The scary part was that she felt right at home.

"I can't explain *myself*, I'm afraid, sir," said Alice, "because I'm not myself, you see."
"I don't see," said the Caterpillar.
—Lewis Carroll (1832–1898)
Alice's Adventures in Wonderland

Curtsy while you're thinking what to say.
It saves time.

One

"Pardon me, but would you have the time?" The voice was harassed and anxious, just like the face Gideon found turned beseechingly up to him. It was an elderly face with wrinkles and a tentative smile, sitting atop a portly body dressed in a plaid suit that combined the improbable colors of lime green and purple.

Somewhat hastily, Gideon looked at his wristwatch. "It's quarter after three," he replied.

"Oh, heavens, I'm late." The little man moaned and bustled away.

Gideon gazed after him for a moment, grappling with the notion that there was something familiar about the preceding scene. He shook off the thought and ventured a few more steps away from his car, looking around him with the wary gaze of a man quite definitely out of his element. Since he was sprung from a long and distinguished line of financial wizards with the Midas touch, his natural habitat tended more toward stately homes, huge boardrooms, and Learjets.

Definitely not seedy carnivals.

Though, to be fair, the colorful jumble of tents, wagons—the horse-drawn kind—people, and animals wasn't exactly seedy, since everything appeared to be clean and in good shape. It was just . . . well, cockeyed. In this age of high-tech special effects the Wonderland carnival was positively archaic. In its thirty years of existence it had eked out a marginal living for its varied dependents without ever making much of a splash. The carnival rolled into small towns and took up temporary residence in a parking lot or empty field for a few days or a week before moving on. The carnival wandered without rhyme or reason. That fact was the major cause of Gideon's apparent short temper. It had taken him nearly a month to find the carnival, and since his task wasn't a particularly pleasant one, the delay had done nothing to improve his state of mind. Muttering to himself, he took several more strides into the heart of chaos and very nearly fell over a towheaded urchin who had appeared out of nowhere.

"You cuss better'n Maggie," the urchin confided with the air bestowing a great compliment.

Estimating the boy's age at six or so, Gideon got a grip on himself and said, "Do you belong here?"

"I'm carny," the boy said, lifting his chin and showing a missing tooth as he grinned.

"Is that your name?"

" 'Course not. My name's Sean." Sean eyed the tall man before him while giving him a disconcertingly adult smile of condescension. "Don't know much, do you? 'Carny' means I belong here. You don't belong here. Whatcha want?"

Unused to children, Gideon returned the stare

for several moments before it occurred to him that he wasn't going to win the battle of wills. Sighing, he said, "I want to talk to the—the manager, I suppose. Whoever runs this place."

"Why dincha say so? Come on, I'll show you." Without waiting for an agreement Sean turned and walked away, his short legs covering the ground with remarkable speed.

Gideon followed as the boy wound his way between wagons and tents and cages. The cages held animals, most of which were sleeping. The variety was astonishing. Gideon counted two lions, a tiger, and what he thought was a cheetah, as well as monkeys, bears, and a number of unidentifiable balls of fur.

He was thinking about the unexpected variety when he rounded the corner of a tent to see Sean holding an earnest conversation with a woman. She turned to face Gideon as he approached—and he felt a jolt as strong as kick in the stomach.

Midtwenties at a guess, though all he was certain of was that childhood was behind her. Her hair was so light it seemed made of spun silver, gleaming in the afternoon sunshine, and it was so long she probably sat on it. Incredibly green eyes looked out of her delicate face with the enigmatic mystery of a cat and an underlying . . . something . . . that wasn't wildness exactly, but more like the mischief of an incorrigible, but delightful, child. And her small, slender body was draped in some filmy green material that fluttered about her in the slight breeze.

If Gideon was any judge of shapely female forms, she was wearing absolutely nothing underneath the gauzy emerald material.

"You're just in time," she told him in a bright, sweet, childlike voice.

Taken aback, Gideon said, "Just in time for wh—" and found himself with an armful of something furry. To his immense relief, he discovered it was a puppy. He stood there holding the small, wriggling creature and feeling slightly shell-shocked as he stared at the woman.

Ignoring him now, she spoke to Sean with improbable sternness. "You should be helping Malcolm get ready. You know he likes tea and poker promptly at four o'clock."

Tea and *crumpets*, Gideon thought. Wasn't it supposed to be tea and *crumpets*? If she'd said *beer* and poker, now he could have understood. He shook the absurd thought away.

"I'll help him, don't I always?" Sean was demanding aggrievedly. "But you said to find Leo and I can't, so I had to tell you. And besides, *he* wanted to talk to you." A small, grubby thumb was jerked toward Gideon.

"Well, all right then." She plucked the puppy from its temporary resting place in Gideon's arms and handed it to the boy. "You take Alexander back to Tina and I'll find Leo."

" 'S okay with me." Sean accepted the puppy with a charitable nod and expertly tucked it under one arm as he strode away.

Gideon discovered that his dark suit was liberally covered with white hair. He brushed at the clinging stuff, then gave up and prepared to address himself to the woman. Except that she was wandering away. He went after her, avoiding one large dog sprawled out between two tents and the ample rump of a huge horse grazing peacefully and completely untethered on thick green grass.

She was standing at the edge of the woods and frowning slightly when he caught up with her.

And before he could say a word, she turned to him with a faintly anxious air.

"Do you think Leo could have gone into the woods? Even after I told him not to?"

He stared down at her, wondering inconsequentially how such a tiny woman could be so . . . so richly curved. Her filmy outfit made the fact obvious. Very obvious. He tried not to think about it. The top of her head didn't even reach to his shoulder, and something about the way she tilted her head to look up at him was peculiarly moving. No. A ridiculous idea.

Then her question sank in. The suspicion that she might be a little less than all there crossed Gideon's mind, but he dismissed it. Those eyes might be enigmatic and contain a gleam of devilment, but there was also sense there. He hoped.

"Who—or what—is Leo?" he asked with what patience he could muster.

"Well, he thinks he's a lion," she explained.

Gideon wasn't sure he wanted to know, but asked anyway, "What is he really?"

Bafflement crossed her features. "We've never been quite sure. Maybe you'll know when you see him."

"I don't think I want to see him. Look, if you run this—this carnival, I came here to talk to you."

"All right," she said mildly. "But first I have to find Leo before he scares somebody. Especially himself."

Gideon discovered he was addressing the back of her silver-blond head as she turned away, and he wasn't surprised to hear a note of frustration in his voice. "At least tell me what the hell he looks like."

When she glanced back over her shoulder at him, he could have sworn there was a fleeting gleam of sheer laughter in her fey eyes, but her sweet voice remained vague. "Oh . . . he's sort of brown. He looks like a cat. But not really. Bigger than a cat. Smaller than a lion."

After that masterly description Gideon was prepared for almost anything. Telling himself that this odd woman was obviously unable to think of anything but her misplaced animal, he got a grip on his patience and began to follow her into the woods.

He lost her almost immediately. It surprised him, because with her silvery hair she should easily have been visible; though shadowed in places, the woods weren't particularly dark. He debated briefly and silently, then cursed under his breath, took his suit jacket off, and rolled up his sleeves. He left his jacket hanging on a handy limb as he set out.

He wasn't worried about becoming lost since he had an excellent sense of direction. And if it occurred to him that the diminutive lady, who, according to Sean, was the manager of Wonderland, would hardly treat him with such childlike friendliness once she found out why he was here, he tried not to think about it. Even though he had an uncomfortable awareness that it was his reason for engaging in this absurd hunt: anything to delay the inevitable.

Being a methodical man, he worked his way methodically through the woods. Bordered on two sides by winding, two-lane country roads with fields beyond, the forest was a roughly triangular section of towering oaks and maples and other hardwoods bisected by a tumbling stream complete with a small waterfall. He estimated the total size of the forest at about ten acres.

He searched ten acres. Then, hot, tired, and irritable, he found himself back where he'd started. His jacket was just where he'd left it. So was something else.

It was crouched on the same limb, the very tips of two forepaws resting on the jacket's collar. It was, without doubt, brown—several mottled shades of brown, in fact. And it was smaller than a lion by several feet and a considerable number of pounds. But it was definitely bigger than a cat. Even though that was what it *was*.

Ridiculously long, funnel-shaped ears topped the traditional wedge-shape of a cat's head. A ringed and bushy tail lay alongside the mottled-brown body with its tip twitching lazily. And huge, startlingly round, yellow eyes peered at Gideon doubtfully.

"Leo?" He felt a bit absurd asking, but something about the hesitant stare made him feel he ought to.

"Wooo?" the animal replied.

Gideon blinked. Not exactly a catlike sound, he reflected. Still, it had to be Leo. And he was sick of the search. "Come down from there," he commanded firmly. Somewhat to his surprise, Leo instantly jumped down from the tree's branch and stood looking up at him with a comically dubious expression on his pointed, furry face.

Gideon lifted his jacket from the limb and draped it over his arm. "Come along," he ordered, and began making his way out of the woods. A glance down showed him that Leo was obediently pacing beside him. He was a large animal; the point of his shoulders nearly reached to Gideon's knee, and he had to be almost three feet long from the tip of his nose to the end of his tail.

"Oh, good! You found him."

For an instant Gideon's feelings threatened to overcome him. She was sitting just outside the woods in cool shade, her seat a canvas camp chair. A bundle of colorful material was in her lap, and she was mending a tear with small, neat stitches. Opening his mouth to say something that probably would have scorched her, Gideon was forestalled when Leo, making the most absurd chattering sounds, hurried over to her.

She seemed to listen seriously, gazing at the cat gravely as he reared up with his forepaws on her knees. Then, when he fell silent and looked at her expectantly, she shook her head and said, "Well, it isn't my fault. I told you not to go into the woods. Tina saved your lunch for you, so go and eat it."

"Wooo?" Leo asked dolefully.

"Yes, I expect so. She has every right to be angry with you. You'd better hurry. If you ask her nicely, she might make you another one."

Leo removed his paws from her knees and loped—peculiarly, since his back legs were longer than his front ones—toward the scattered wagons.

Gideon gazed after him for a long, silent moment, then looked down at the woman. "Make him another what?"

"Collar." She held her sewing up and studied it critically, then neatly finished off the row of stitches and removed the needle from the cloth, tucking it away in a small sewing kit, which she slid absently into a pocket of her skirt. "He lost his in the woods. Didn't you hear him say so?"

Several possible responses to that mild question occurred to him as he watched her rise and fold the camp chair, then tuck it under one arm along with the bundle of material. Gideon really—*really*—wanted to believe that this woman was absolutely batty. It was the simplest and safest explanation. She was quite mad, and it would be in his best interests to say what he'd come to say and then leave this place with all speed.

He half convinced himself of that. Then she looked up at him, brows slightly raised in question. And he felt a curious mixture of shock and satisfaction when he saw a brief glimpse of cool, tranquil intelligence in her green eyes.

She was not crazy.

Gideon had always been fascinated by puzzles. He couldn't leave one unsolved; he had to understand. He rediscovered the trait within himself at that moment. This woman was the most enigmatic puzzle he'd ever stumbled across, and he couldn't leave without at least trying to understand her.

That's what he told himself.

"How did you scratch your arm?" she asked, looking at a small cut on his forearm.

He followed her gaze, remembering that he'd rolled up his sleeves at some point. "Thorns, I suppose. Do you mind telling me your name?"

"No. It's Maggie. We should put some antiseptic on that so it won't get infected. My wagon's this way."

Walking beside her, he glanced down and had to ask. "Did you really understand Leo?"

"Didn't you?"

He decided not to answer that. "Maggie what?"

"Durant."

"My name's Gideon Hughes."

"Yes," she said tranquilly. "I know."

"You do?" He was a little startled.

"Of course. Balthazar's attorney contacted us after the tragedy so we'd know what had happened. Sad, isn't it? That he went all that way, I mean, and almost made it. If the authorities hadn't stopped him in Dakar, the rhino would never have gotten so upset and gored him. But you can't get probate for months, so we weren't really expecting you yet."

Her gentle, childlike voice was disarming; it took Gideon several moments to digest what she'd told him. "Expecting me?" he ventured finally.

"Naturally."

Gideon was about to question her further when they rounded the back of one of the wagons and saw something that made him forget everything else.

The carnival was camped along the edge of the forest about a hundred yards from the road so that several of the wagons and tents could take advantage of the shade. Between a faded pink tent and a mauve-colored wagon, a red-and-blue-checked circular tablecloth had been spread on the ground in the shade. Around the edges of the cloth were five people frowning in concentration at the cards they held in their hands.

Only one of them looked familiar to Gideon; he was the absurdly dressed man who had asked the time. By comparison, he didn't look so ridiculous now. On his left was a lean, aristocratic gentleman with fine silver hair who seemed to be wearing a white toga. Clockwise around the circle, next was a clown in full makeup and costume, a woman with wild black hair dressed colorfully as a gypsy, and a redheaded man somewhere in his twenties who was wearing a Scottish kilt and a garland of wildflowers in his hair.

Gideon stopped in his tracks and stared at them. The tablecloth was covered with the remnants of tea, complete with a delicate pot and dainty cups and saucers as well as a number of plates holding nothing but crumbs. The clown had a monkey on his shoulder that was busily eating a banana, a cockatoo roosted on the shoulder of the toga-clad man, and Leo was chattering insistently in the ear of the gypsy.

"Go away!" she muttered, elbowing him sharply.

"Bet, Tina," the toga-clad man said in an irritable tone.

"Can't you see I'm trying—" She turned her head to glare at the persistent cat, finally holding her cards down close to his nose. "Look at this!"

Leo peered, then emitted a squeak and hastily sat down.

"Fold," the four men chorused instantly as they tossed their cards down.

Tina looked at the small pile of pennies in the center of the tablecloth, then turned her head again to glare at Leo. "I'll give you a collar," she said. "How do you feel about a hangman's noose?"

Leo said, "Wooo," miserably, and hung his head.

Gideon shook himself out of the stupor and continued walking, finding Maggie waiting patiently at a huge wagon some little distance from the others. He hardly looked at the wagon. Jerking a thumb backward, he asked incredulously, "Are they kidding?"

She looked past him at the tea-and-poker party, then lifted her puzzled gaze to his face. "About what?"

He stared down into utterly limpid green eyes.

She was very lovely. He decided he should leave. Immediately. Her eyes were like wells, so deep he could only see the placid surface reflecting light and just hinting at all the possibilities of what might lie underneath. Treasures were hidden in wells. It was also possible, he reminded himself, for one to drown in them.

"Never mind," he murmured. "I don't think it matters."

For an instant, so brief he might have imagined it, he saw again that flash of sheer intelligence, the utterly rational and shrewd humor. Then the surface of her gaze was unbroken once more, serene and without even ripples to hint at things moving in unseen depths. Her smile was warm, like sunlight through a cloud, catching at his breath.

"This is my wagon." She turned and climbed the steps to the open door.

Gideon felt bereft for a moment, rudderless. It wasn't a comfortable sensation for a man of thirty-five, especially when that man had never taken an unplanned turn in his life. But a small voice in his mind whispered now, seductively, that treasures weren't found on the predictable and neatly paved walkways where a thousand feet passed daily. He tried to ignore the voice; he'd never heard the damned thing before, and it promised, at the very least, a lack of control that appalled him.

"Gideon?" She looked out at him, brows lifted. "Aren't you coming in?"

After a moment he climbed the steps and went into her wagon.

"Sit down," she invited, gesturing toward a brightly green love seat as she leaned the camp chair against the wall, put the bundle of cloth on the foot of the bed, and opened the door of a big wardrobe to begin searching through it.

He was glad to sit. The interior of the wagon struck his senses like a blow. He looked around slowly, his gaze lingering on the scarlet velvet bedspread and tasseled pillows covering the bed that took up most of the space. He closed his eyes, opening them again when she settled beside him. She was holding a first-aid box open on her lap.

While he watched silently, she got out a tube of antiseptic and some gauze and put the box on the floor, then took his wrist and guided his arm until it rested across her thighs. He could feel the warmth of her, and a soft scent like wildflowers in a meadow rose to his nostrils. Her long, clever fingers were bare of rings.

"Are you married?" he asked.

She was carefully spreading antiseptic cream over the scratch on his arm and didn't look up. "No."

"Involved with anyone?"

"No. Are you?"

He gazed at her profile and felt more then heard a sigh escape him. "I wasn't when I got here."

Finished with her task, she tossed the used gauze into a small trash can near the door. "It'll heal better if it isn't covered," she said, capping the tube of cream.

"Did you hear what I said?" he demanded.

"Yes." She put the tube back into the box and then sat back, looking at him. A tiny smile curved her lips and her fey eyes were completely unreadable.

"I just made a verbal pass," he explained.

She considered the matter, then shook her head. "No. You indicated interest. A verbal pass is something like—'Why don't we have breakfast in bed?' "

"Why don't we have breakfast in bed?"

"You do come straight to the point, don't you?"

He eyed her, a little amused at both of them, and very surprised at himself. It was totally unlike him to move so fast, and even less like him to be so blunt. Still, having begun in that vein, he kept going. "We're both over twenty-one. At least, I hope—?"

"I'm twenty-eight," she supplied sedately.

"Then you've certainly heard quite a few verbal passes."

"A few."

He wanted to ask how she had responded to passes from other men, but bit back the question. She would say it was none of his business —or, at least, any other woman would. And she'd be right. Her past was no concern of his, and that had never troubled him in previous relationships with women; in fact, he'd never even been tempted to ask.

"Are you just going to ignore my pass?" he asked.

She looked at him, an uncomfortable perception surfacing in her vivid eyes. Rising up out of the depths, he thought, like some mysterious, all-knowing siren. "Unless and until your motives change, yes, I think I will."

"My motives?"

Mildly she said, "You don't like giving up control to anyone else, and as long as you don't understand me, you feel it puts me in control. You don't want the vulnerability of a possible relationship, just the control of knowledge. Sex, you believe, is a means to finding that knowledge. In your experience, women tend to give up all that they are to a lover, whether he responds in kind or not. How am I doing?"

Gideon cleared his throat and leaned back in the corner of the love seat, removing his arm from her warm thighs. He devoutly hoped he didn't look as unnerved as he felt. She had neatly—and with devastating accuracy—stripped his motives bare while becoming even more of an enigma herself. "That makes me sound like a selfish bastard, doesn't it?" he said, neither admitting nor denying what she'd said.

"Most people are selfish; it's the nature of the beast. You have a logical mind and it's perfectly logical to think that the shortest distance between two points is a straight line."

"Are you saying it isn't?"

In a very gentle voice she said, "Not between people. Between people, shortcuts are usually painful."

She was right—and he was even more surprised at himself. Did he really feel so out of control? Had he been so shaken by his confused response to her that his first instinct had been to reach for an immediate, shallow intimacy? Such an abrupt leap, assuming she had accepted, virtually guaranteed that there would be little more than a brief fling between them. Because she was right about something else; intimacy without knowledge was seldom anything but damaging.

And he *knew* that.

After a moment he said, "I apologize."

Maggie looked faintly surprised. "I wasn't offended. I just want you to understand that I don't believe sex is a means to an end. By the time two people become that intimate, most of the questions should already be answered."

"You're right." Gideon was mildly surprised at his own lack of defensiveness; he was, more than anything, intrigued by her insight into his motives, and disturbed by those motives themselves. "But how did you know? About me, I mean. Did it show so plainly?"

"No. I just knew."

Now, that *was* unnerving, he thought. "How?"

"It's a knack I have," she answered serenely.

Before Gideon could probe further, there was a thud near the door that might have been a knock, and the redhead member of the tea party, the garland of flowers still in his hair, peered in at them and spoke in an aggrieved tone with a touch of Scotland in the rhythm.

"Maggie, love, you've got to do something about Oswald! He's taken them again."

She turned her head to look at the visitor. "Farley, I can't teach Oswald to love bagpipes. And I can't keep him from hiding them from you. Why don't you challenge him to a poker game and bet the pipes? He always loses to you."

Farley brightened. "That's a thought, it is indeed, love. It'll appeal to his sense of honor, what's more."

"Of course it will. Farley, this is Gideon."

"Hello," Farley said briefly to the other man, and then vanished from the doorway.

Gideon told himself silently that endearments probably came naturally to Farley; it didn't mean a thing.

Maggie apparently considered their previous conversation over, because she picked up the first-aid box and rose to her feet. She put the box away in the big wardrobe, then came back around the foot of the bed and looked at Gideon with a faint smile. "Do you want to go meet the other people you'll be putting out of work?"

He blinked, the attack totally unexpected. Not that it *was* an attack, exactly; her voice remained sweet and calm. But the words . . . Getting to his feet, he said slowly, "You obviously know I mean to sell the carnival."

"Yes. Natural, I suppose. Our income barely covers expenses, and we could by no stretch of the imagination be a tax write-off. You aren't carny, so you have no feeling for this life or what it means to the people involved. I understand Balthasar was such a distant connection you aren't certain how you were related to him, so no family feeling is involved."

Gideon opened his mouth, but she was going on in the same soft, childlike voice.

"The wagons are all antiques and will probably fetch a healthy price. Trained animals are always in demand, and those that don't perform can certainly go to zoos. We have a number of costumes and carnival games you can doubtless unload for a few dollars. You won't have to worry about severance pay, of course, or retirement benefits or pension plans; carnies don't sign employment agreements. So it doesn't really matter that most of the people here quite literally have no place else to go, or that at least three of them were born in Wonderland wagons. That certainly isn't your problem."

*At least I knew who I was
when I got up this morning,
but I think I must have been changed
several times since then.*

Two

She was still an enigma, but Gideon now knew
at least one thing about her: She could flay the
bark off an oak tree without raising her voice or
losing her gentle smile. He felt a bit flayed and—
now—defensive.

"What do you expect me to do?" he demanded.
"I don't know a damned thing about carnivals,
and I have no desire to own one."

"Of course not. Along with the other drawbacks,
it's a totally alien way of life to you. I expect you're
doing the only reasonable thing to be done."

Her voice was unchanged, and her agreement
held no sarcasm whatsoever, but for some reason
Gideon felt even worse about the situation. "What
will you do?" he asked, unable to halt the question.

"Unlike the others, I do have somewhere else to
go."

"Where?"

"That isn't your concern. Do you want to meet
the others now, or shall I break the news to them
myself?"

Gideon wanted to shake her. He wanted to kiss her. She stood in her ridiculous wagon telling him things he didn't want to hear in her sweet voice, looking up at him with her enigmatic, haunting eyes. And he was still intrigued by her, dammit, even more than ever.

Realizing that he badly needed to think this through before he made a total fool of himself, he said tightly, "It's getting late. I'll stay in town tonight and come back in the morning. I'll meet the others then."

"As you wish."

He hesitated, then asked unwillingly, "You'll be here, won't you?"

She chose to answer the question generally, though it had been directed specifically at her. "We'll be here."

Gideon hesitated again, then swore beneath his breath and left the wagon.

Maggie stepped to the doorway and leaned against one side, gazing after him. His tall form moved with natural grace, she noted idly, and with the unthinking power that came not only from physical strength but from intellectual and emotional certainty; Gideon Hughes had always known exactly who and what he was.

Farley appeared around the end of the wagon and followed her gaze. "Where's he going?"

"Town. But he'll be back," she said absently.

"Tomorrow?"

"No. Tonight. No room at the inn."

Farley looked up at her quizzically. "Want me to pitch the extra tent?"

"I suppose you'd better." She waited until he began to turn away, then spoke mildly. "Farley? You've never called me love until a few minutes ago."

He looked at her, hazel eyes bright with laughter. "The mood just took me," he explained innocently.

"Anything in particular spur the mood?" she asked.

"I expect it's a dog-in-the-manger attitude," he said in a judicious tone, then winked at her and turned away.

Maggie looked after him until he was out of her sight, then murmured to herself, "You were listening, Farley; I really wish you hadn't done that." After a moment she glanced toward the settling cloud of dust that Gideon's departure had created, then said even more softly, "And you showed up before I was ready for you. What am I supposed to do now? Damn."

Not quite what she had expected, Mr. Gideon Hughes. There was . . . well, too much of him. Too much physical presence, too much intelligence and perception, and too many plans she couldn't let him discuss with the others. It would be better all around, she thought, if she made him so mad he'd just leave.

He had the look of a man with a formidable temper, which didn't disturb Maggie at all; she had yet to encounter a temper unruly enough to trigger her own. The only problem with that option was that she doubted he'd leave no matter how mad she made him; he certainly hadn't bothered to hide his interest in her, and he also had the look of a man accustomed to getting what he wanted whether it required patience or a pitched battle.

He was less likely to concentrate on dismantling the carnival while in the midst of a pitched battle, of course.

Farley reappeared with an armful of canvas and poles. "Where d'you want it?" he asked cheerfully.

Maggie pointed to a cleared space near her wagon. "There, I suppose." She ignored his raised eyebrows and watched as he began setting up the tent.

It was almost dark when Gideon returned to the carnival's campsite. He didn't know quite how he felt about the fact that renovations in one of the town's two motels and a regional businessman's convention in the other had made getting a room impossible; after his earlier encounter with Maggie he was uncertain of his welcome since he didn't dare guess how she'd feel about his return.

He parked his car nearer her wagon than before and approached it a bit warily. The campsite was relatively quiet; lights and voices came from most of the wagons and several tents, along with the appetizing scents of cooking, but he didn't see anyone moving around outside. A new tent, a hideous yellow color, had been pitched about twelve feet from Maggie's wagon, and Gideon averted his eyes from it.

"Back so soon?" Despite her question, he had the notion that she wasn't at all surprised to see him.

He stopped at the bottom of the steps leading to her door and gazed up at Maggie as she stood in the doorway. Soft light from an oil lamp inside the wagon silhouetted her slender figure and turned the diaphanous dress she wore into little more than a gauzy veil. All his senses responded instantly to the sight of her, and he had to force himself to concentrate on what he was saying. "I couldn't get a room in town," he explained, and hesitated briefly before going on. "Since it's only for one night, I thought I could stay here. If you don't mind."

"This is your carnival," she pointed out mildly. "The wagons are all occupied, but if you'd like to kick somebody out—"

"No, dammit!" Gideon was feeling defensive again and didn't care for the emotion. "If there's no extra room in a wagon or tent, I'll sleep in the car."

Maggie left the doorway and moved to sit on the third step. Her expression was still polite, and her voice was serene when she said, "As a matter of fact we do have an empty tent. The yellow one there. You're welcome to it."

Before he could speak, Gideon caught a hint of motion behind her, and even as a loud thud shook the wagon he realized that the bed had fallen.

Maggie didn't even flinch.

"What the hell?"

"Defective catch," she said. "The bed is supposed to stay up against the wall. Like beds in trains. But the catch has a mind of its own. Are you going to take the tent?"

"Yes." He could, he decided, accept the unexpected calmly. Of course he could. "Thank you."

"Why thank me? It's your tent."

He took a breath and folded his arms across his chest. "Tell me something. Are we going to go on this way?"

"This way?" Her eyes reflected the last of the daylight like some shaded forest pool.

"Yes, Miss Durant, this way. You're hell-bent to keep needling me about my plans for the carnival, aren't you?"

Without replying to his question she said, "Tell me something?"

"If I can."

"Are your plans set in concrete?"

"No," he said after a moment. "I try never to do that. Do you want an opportunity to argue for the defense?"

"I think I do," she said slowly, looking at him with a very slight frown that stole the fey innocence from her face and lent it an expression of troubled gravity. "But if you're planning to leave tomorrow, that doesn't give me much time."

Since Gideon had mentally been searching for an excuse to spend more time with her, the opportunity was too good to pass up. "I can stay a few days. If I have to."

The reflective green eyes looked at him with a sudden gleam of irony in their depths. "Don't go to any trouble on my account," she said gently.

Gideon cleared his throat and tried not to look as sheepish as he felt. Blast the woman, she was continually cutting him down to size. "Sorry. That remark was in the nature of protective coloration. A man isn't supposed to jump at the slightest excuse to be near a woman."

With an interested lift to her brows she said, "Who says he isn't supposed to?"

"It's in the macho handbook. Between chapters on why real men don't eat quiche or wear pink shirts." He wasn't terribly surprised that she seemed neither flattered nor insulted by his admitted interest in her, since she understood his motives all too well.

"If I were you," she said, "I'd throw out that particular handbook."

"Are we back to being sensitive again? I've lost

track." The note of despair in his voice wasn't entirely false.

Maggie's mouth curved slightly. "God knows what the current phase is, but I prefer honesty. Just be yourself."

"I was being myself," he said, "earlier. And you as good as told me I was a selfish bastard."

"You said that, not me. All I said was that you wanted to control the situation," she pointed out in a tone of tranquil innocence.

He sighed. "I have the unnerving feeling that my chances of besting you conversationally are nil."

Her smile widened, her exotic eyes holding a gleam of genuine amusement. "I hate to lose," she murmured. "You might want to keep that in mind." Without a change in tone she added, "There are a couple of blankets in the tent; if you need more, I have a few extra ones. Have you eaten?"

"No."

"Tina's our cook this week; she's fixing a pot of Irish stew, I believe. Would you like some?"

"Please."

Maggie nodded and got to her feet. "We usually eat in our own wagons, so I'll go and get the food while you change. You are going to change, aren't you?"

He glanced down at his neat three-piece suit. "Slightly out of place, am I?"

"A rose among daisies."

"No man," he said after a stunned instant, "likes to be called a rose. And that isn't from the handbook; that's in the marrow. Luckily, I brought a few things more casual than what I have on." He eyed the yellow tent with a certain amount of ungrateful revulsion. "I won't be able to stand up in there, let alone change clothes. May I borrow your wagon for a few minutes?"

"Certainly." She descended the remaining steps until she stood before him. "I have to check the animals before dark anyway. Make yourself at home."

Gideon watched her walk away, idly trying to decide why she seemed to move more gracefully than any other woman he could recall. A dancer, perhaps? No, he didn't think so. Her grace was innate rather than taught, like that of some wild creature. In fact, he thought that was what intrigued him about her more than anything else. In her movements, her voice and eyes, even her quiet glances and slow smiles, there was a sense of something . . . not quite tamed.

His imagination, perhaps. But he didn't think so. Whatever it was, he knew only that he had never sensed it in a woman before, and that his response to it was instinctive and emotional rather than intellectual. Just like his aversion to being called a rose, it was something as deep as his marrow.

Which was not to say that he didn't respond to her on both intellectual and emotional levels as well. He did. He enjoyed talking to her—or rather, sparring with her. He felt unusually aware of his own senses when she was near, and he was also, he'd noticed, more apt to say exactly what he was thinking without feeling any need to hold back or guard his words.

Frowning, Gideon turned away from the wagon and toward his car. He was still conscious of not being in control of this situation, of being off balance and out of his element; that was largely due to Maggie but not entirely.

A rose among daisies. Great.

Leo was sitting on the hood of his rental car. They stared at each other through the deepening twilight, the cat still doubtful and the man likewise.

"Wooo?" Leo ventured.

Gideon felt an absurd urge to reply, but he had no idea what the question was. Opting for silence, he got his bag out of the trunk and then locked up the car and returned to Maggie's wagon to change. By the time she came back around half an hour later, he was dressed in jeans and a pale brown sweater and was sitting on the green love seat looking through a heavy volume of English literature. He set the book aside quickly when he saw her and rose to take a crowded wooden tray from her.

"Let me."

"I'm not proud," she said, relinquishing the tray. "Wait a second while I get the table out."

Gideon watched her unearth a card table from the big wardrobe and unfold it near the love seat. While she was doing that, she said, "By the way, we have a bathhouse set up at the other end of camp in one of the bigger tents. All the modern conveniences. Except hot water."

He thought of shaving in cold water and couldn't help but grimace. "Do you people always live like this?"

She unloaded the tray while he held it, placing dishes of hot stew, a basket of bread, pitcher of iced tea, glasses, napkins, and cutlery onto the card table. "Always? I suppose. We were to have set up closer to town, but a bigger carnival got in ahead of us, so there wasn't much use. Our next stop will probably be Wichita, but a circus was there last week, so we should wait a few weeks before we go in. That's why we're camping here, really."

"Ever thought about scheduling regular stops?"

"Schedules are so—so rigid. Don't you think?" She moved around the table and sat down at one end of the love seat. "Just put the tray on the bed."

He obeyed, wondering if the comment about rigid schedules had been aimed at him. Taking his place beside her, he said, "I suppose you know I'm a banker?"

She poured a glass of tea for him and sent him a glance of amusement. "An investment banker, I believe. Which basically means that you gamble huge sums of money."

"Not at all. I provide financial backing for business ventures."

"Which could well fail."

"It's a possibility," he admitted. "But not that much of a gamble. I make sure the risk is minimal."

"I'll bet you do," she murmured.

Gideon decided to change the subject; this one was making him sound and feel like the proverbial stuffy banker. Nodding toward the table beside the love seat where he'd put the literature book, he said, "I think that's the textbook I remember from college. Yours?"

"Yes."

"What did you major in?"

"Psychology, history, and computer technology." He blinked. "What, all three?"

"Three different colleges." Her voice was placid. "I can usually earn a four-year degree in two years. Next fall I'll try my hand at archaeology. Very interesting, the study of man. I always had a fondness for pyramids—maybe I'll specialize in Egyptian archaeology."

Gideon ate in silence for a few moments, vaguely aware that the stew was excellent. "You mean you have three four-year degrees?"

"So far."

"And you earned them while running a carnival?"

Maggie looked faintly surprised. "No, I'm just managing the carnival this summer. Before he went off to Africa, Balthasar asked me to. I didn't have anything else planned."

"Three degrees, and she's running a sideshow," Gideon murmured to himself.

She glanced at him again, then said, "When my father died, he left a trust fund for me and asked that I use the money for my education. I like learning, and I haven't run out of money yet, so I'm still in school. I suppose you could call me a habitual student." Quite abruptly, her soft voice took on a steely note. "As for sideshows—there are no freaks here. No con men or rigged games. Just a group of mildly eccentric people who happen to be quite nice on the whole, and who don't know any other way to live."

Gideon sat back in his corner of the love seat and looked at her. "I keep saying the wrong thing, don't I?"

She matched his pose, leaning back in her own corner. "I think you're trying to find some logic in this situation." Her tone was dispassionate rather than forgiving.

"Will I?"

"No. The carnival isn't logical, as you understand logic. Nor are the people here—including me. Your world is a million miles away."

He shook his head. "I'm not that different. I haven't dropped onto an alien planet, Maggie."

She smiled. "No. And this *is* Kansas, not Oz.

But you expect order, and you aren't going to find that here. No schedules—except for Malcolm's tea parties. It's a place where you can wear a clown's face, or a toga or a kilt, and nobody looks twice. A place where you talk to the animals and they talk back, and it doesn't matter that you aren't speaking the same language. A place where being normal is to be slightly mad."

"There are lunatics in my world," he pointed out.

"Yes. But in your world, they aren't normal. In this world, they are." She was on the end of the love seat with the lamp beside it, and the soft glow made her hair gleam silver. Gideon thought she looked like an angel—except for the strange and enigmatic depth of her eyes.

A mad angel.

He cleared his throat. "Are we talking about the carnival? Or about us?"

Maggie looked at him steadily. "Us? Didn't we close that subject?"

"No. If I remember, you used the words 'unless and until' my motives change. They have." He was surprised to hear himself say that, but wasn't tempted to take back the statement.

"What are your motives now?"

"I thought you had a knack of seeing things like that?" he murmured.

"If you expect me to be consistent," she said somewhat dryly, "you haven't been listening to me."

"Sorry." He had to smile a little. "All right, then. My motives. I won't deny that I was—knocked off balance earlier today, or that you were right about my motives then. But I agree with what you said. Most of the questions should be answered first.

I'd like to try to get those answers, and control has nothing to do with it. I want you, Maggie."

To his surprise, the blunt statement drew a visible reaction from her. Her eyes widened and . . . she blushed. *Blushed.* Faint color flowed over her cheekbones like a delicate tide, making her appear very young and adorably confused. It was fascinating to watch.

"I see," she murmured, her gaze falling.

"Are you blushing?" He sounded as astonished as he felt.

"Of course not. I outgrew that years ago." She looked back at him, mysterious ripples disturbing the serenity of her eyes. "I was just surprised."

"Why? You knew I wanted you."

Maggie didn't want to answer his question, partly because she thought her answer might well make him draw away. It was obvious that he hadn't heard his own voice, hadn't been aware of the implacable note in it. When he had said he wanted her, there had been more than desire in his voice, something unrelenting as if it came from instinct. And whatever it was, her response to it had caught her completely off guard.

The sensation was strange, almost frightening. She could feel her heart beating, thudding against her ribs and in her throat in an uneven rhythm. Her skin felt hot, and she was suddenly, vividly aware of her body as being female. The cool rationality of her mind had become uncertainty and confusion.

Always before, Maggie had felt detached from men. She had heard a number of men express interest and desire, men who, like Gideon, had questions because they were puzzled by her. Yet none of them had roused the slightest spark of response in her, and she had not gone out of her way to supply answers. Never one to accept half measures, she had long ago decided that if she didn't find the *right* man, she wouldn't make the mistake of settling for the wrong one. She had flirted, enjoying the verbal sparring—much as she had with Gideon. She had never been tempted to go beyond flirting. Until now.

"Maggie?"

She looked at him. Really looked. Less formal now in his jeans and sweater. His thick copper hair gleamed with gold highlights, and his eyes were the gray of storm clouds. His face was almost classically handsome, strong and filled with character. The pale brown sweater set off his tan and made the power of broad shoulders more evident, and the jeans fit well over narrow hips and long legs. He was curiously more masculine than any man she'd ever met, as if an aura surrounded him.

He leaned toward her. "Maggie?"

She drew a breath, wondering idly when that automatic function had become a voluntary thing. "Are you sure you want your answers?" she asked huskily.

"Why wouldn't I?"

"You may not like them." She had often thought of herself as an odd woman in many ways; that had never troubled her, but it could well disturb him.

"I can't imagine that," he said. "But it doesn't matter. It's too late for me to make the choice, Maggie. You can throw me out, but I can't walk away."

"I can't throw you out. This is your carnival."

"Stop saying that." His voice was sharp. "I'm not talking about the carnival, and you know it."

After a moment she half nodded, realizing that the choice had been made for her as well. The timing couldn't have been worse, and she was aware for the first time of just how painful it would be if the man whose questions she *wanted* to answer didn't like the answers at all. When he began to understand her, he could well decide that their worlds were indeed too far apart. Or he could, in the end, want only an affair to satisfy a purely physical desire. Only time would tell.

"I suppose—" She was interrupted by a rap somewhere near the door.

The woman dressed so colorfully as a gypsy, her black hair in wild ringlets, stuck her head in the doorway. "I thought I'd get the tray if you two are finished," she said briskly.

Maggie glanced at Gideon, then said, "We're finished. But you didn't have to come for it, Tina."

"No trouble." She came into the wagon and began transferring everything from the card table to the tray on the bed.

"Tina, this is Gideon."

"Of course it is," Tina said before Gideon could say a word. She eyed him, then looked at Maggie. "His feet'll stick out," she observed.

"Not if he bends his knees," Maggie said.

• "That's true." Tina lifted the tray easily, her gaze still on Maggie. "Lamont lost his nose," she said with the clear expectation of being understood.

"Where?"

"He doesn't know. But he's upset."

Maggie nodded. "Okay. I'll go talk to him."

Tina nodded in turn, then briskly carried the tray out of the wagon.

For a long moment after she left, Gideon didn't say a word. Then, very carefully, he said, "I gather my feet will stick out of the tent unless I bend my knees?"

Maggie was looking at him solemnly, apparently back on balance now. "Yes."

"So far so good. I hope Lamont is the clown?"

"He is."

Gideon sighed. "I don't know whether to be glad or terrified that I understood that conversation."

"Let me know when you make up your mind."

He looked at her. "You were about to say something before Tina came in."

"Was I?" Oh. I think I was about to say that the subject was open again."

"The subject of us?"

Maggie got to her feet and began folding up the card table. "That subject, yes. At the moment, however, I have to go see a clown about his nose."

"It's still early," Gideon ventured, watching her.

"I get up at dawn to feed the animals."

He sighed. "And tomorrow's another day."

"Good night, Gideon."

"I think it's obvious," Farley said in a firm tone. "Maggie's snuggling up to the man so he won't break us up."

Tina threw him a warning glance, but Sean, who was sitting in the doorway of the wagon finishing his stew, didn't even glance at the two adults inside. "Watch what you say," Tina ordered in a low, fierce voice.

"The lad isn't paying attention—"

"She likes him," Sean said.

Tina looked at Farley. "He *always* pays attention." Then she looked back at her son. "Why do you think she likes him, Sean?"

The boy shrugged. "Dunno. When he left today, she was lookin' after him. Maybe that. Can I sleep in Buster's tent, Ma? He's got Alexander with him, and—"

"All right, but I'd better not catch you roaming around outside."

Wise in the ways of his parent, Sean vanished from the doorway before she could change her mind, leaving his plate balanced precariously on the threshold.

"D'you think the lad's right?" Farley asked, lounging back on the daybed that was wedged in between the door and the table where Tina was stacking the washed dishes.

She half shrugged. "He's a good-looking devil, and he can't keep his eyes off her. Judging by his clothes, I doubt he needs the money he'd get from selling out. If he wants to get in good with Maggie, he won't make that threat. We'll see."

After a moment Farley said, "So we be nice to the man and wait? I've never been one for patience."

"What else can we do? As soon as he gets probate, he can sell out. We can't stop him."

"Can't we, now? I'm thinking there's always a way of doing that. A man isn't a mountain, but they have one thing in common. They can both be got around."

Tina leaned back against the table and looked at him. "You could talk most devils out of both horns and at least one cloven hoof, Farley, but don't try your tricks on that one. Maggie has a chance of getting round him, but the rest of us haven't a hope in hell. Now, would you mind very much getting out from underfoot so I can finish my work?"

He rose with an injured expression. "You don't have to throw me out, I was leaving."

Maggie remained in the darkness close to Tina's caravan until she was sure Farley was gone, then eased away in silence and moved toward her own wagon. She had listened to at least two other conversations tonight, and all were basically the same. Everyone was nervous about Gideon, but convinced that she would either charm or seduce him into sparing the carnival.

Which gave her, she hoped, a little more time.

What she had to avoid at all costs was for Gideon to announce to the others that he meant to sell. Until he committed himself to that plan, she thought nothing would happen—at least for a few days. The level of tension was too high now, so she couldn't expect more than a few days' grace no matter what he did.

She had considered telling him the truth, but had discarded the idea at least for the moment. She didn't know him yet, and in any case, hearing that he had inherited along with the carnival one murderer was apt to upset him a bit.

Feeling restless and uneasy, she returned to her wagon, skirting Gideon's tent. A faint light from the small oil lamp Farley had left glowed inside it, but there was no shadow to indicate if Gideon was awake or sleeping. Maggie climbed into her wagon and softly closed the door.

She changed into her usual sleepwear and then moved the lamp and its small table beside her bed. In the few weeks she'd been here, she had grown more or less accustomed to the scarlet velvet bedspread and gold-tasseled pillows, so she didn't think about how they looked. And she didn't think about how she looked lying back on the pillows in her white teddy with the book of literature in her lap. Since a tacit rule of the carnies was that no one was needlessly disturbed once their door or tent flap was closed at night, she wasn't expecting visitors.

It was a habit of hers to read before sleeping, usually old favorites, and the collection of poems, short stories, and essays was perfect. She was immersed in one long, rambling poem when the tap came at her door, and she answered absently.

"Yes?"

The door opened. "I wanted to take you up on your offer," Gideon began, stepping inside.

For one very long moment Maggie wasn't sure which offer he was talking about. She was hardly a shy woman, but even in the lamplight the intensity of his gaze was obvious, and she was suddenly very conscious of her brief and quite revealing choice of sleepwear. Then she remembered.

"Oh. The extra blankets?"

In some rational part of his mind Gideon had questioned his own attraction to this fey woman. It wasn't her beauty, he had thought; he wasn't particularly susceptible to feminine beauty, having discovered long ago that the enduring traits were the inner ones. Though now, at this moment, he wasn't so sure. She was wearing a white teddy with a deep V neckline and a gauzy lace panel at the waist, below which was the briefest skirt he'd ever seen. Her knees were slightly raised to provide a prop for the book in her lap, and her long hair had been pulled around over her shoulder to drift over one breast like strands of silk.

Curiously enough, the gaudy, even tawdry, bed had become something entirely different now. The scarlet spread seemed deeper in color, the tasseled pillows bright splashes of color. She glowed in the center like some rare jewel.

He couldn't stop looking at her. Wanting her.

"The blankets?" she repeated.

Gideon cleared his throat. "Right. The blankets."

"Top shelf of the wardrobe."

He took a step, intending to walk around the foot of the bed to reach the wardrobe. But somehow, he found himself sitting on the bed beside her. She was looking at him gravely, faint color in her cheeks, and her voice was a little husky when she spoke.

"I don't think this is a very good idea."

"It feels like a good idea," he murmured, lifting one hand to cup her cheek. "I've wanted to kiss you since the first moment you turned and looked at me."

"Is that all you want?" she murmured. "A kiss?"

"You know better. But I'll settle for that. At least as a start."

Maggie didn't protest again. She admitted to herself only as his lips touched hers that this was something she wanted, even something she needed. Then her reasons didn't seem to matter very much.

The first touch was gentle, almost tentative, but the hesitancy vanished quickly. Burned away. Maggie could feel the heat rise in her like a storm surge, so swift and violent she had no defense against it. His mouth hardened, slanting across hers to deepen the kiss with a stark passion that made her shudder helplessly, and she was barely aware when her arms lifted of their own volition to encircle his neck.

*"She's in that state of mind," said
the White Queen, "that she wants to deny
something—only she doesn't know what
to deny!"*

Three

Her arms around his neck . . . It was that mind-
less gesture of trust and desire that brought some
semblance of sanity back to Maggie. She felt the
thick softness of his hair beneath her fingers, felt
the hard pressure of his chest against her breasts
as he drew her suddenly closer, and she was conscious of the same shock she'd felt earlier.

She wanted him. Questions didn't matter. Answers didn't matter. What she felt was something
so deep there wasn't even a word to name it.
All she knew for certain was that now she understood what true madness felt like.

It was Gideon who ended the kiss with visible
reluctance, raising his head slightly to look at
her. His eyes were heavy lidded and darkened, his
face taut. "I didn't expect that," he murmured.

She had to swallow before she could get the
question out. "Expect what?"

"Didn't you feel it too? The power of it?"

Maggie was an honest woman, but she also had
a strong sense of self-preservation. At that mo-

ment she decided a truthful answer might be gasoline thrown on the fire. Unless, of course, she could turn an emotional reality into an impersonal observation. In the most even voice she could manage, she said, "If you drop the right two chemicals into a beaker, sometimes you get quite a reaction."

"So we're just two chemicals that happen to react to each other?" His voice was level.

"Physically, yes." She didn't believe that, but elected to take some kind of stand; if nothing else, it would give them something to argue about. "The easy way, remember? The shortcut. If you push the right buttons physically, you're going to get a predictable response. An emotional response is another matter altogether." Her throat was aching, but she met his narrowing gaze with certainty in her own.

Somewhat belatedly she mentally ordered her fingers to leave his hair alone and drew her arms from around his neck.

After a moment Gideon removed his own arms and straightened, but continued to look down at her. The flicker of anger she'd seen in his eyes had been fleeting, replaced now by a considering look that was a bit too perceptive for her peace of mind.

"Is this where I get mad and storm out?" he asked.

Maggie had become accustomed to the fact that she often baffled people, but she could never understand why. Now she knew. It was somewhat unnerving and rather fascinating to have a person's shrewd comprehension turned on her for a change. But stubbornly, she stuck to her part.

"That's up to you," she told him. She'd never

even considered how difficult it would be to sound dignified while wearing a scanty white teddy. She made a mental note to herself to consider the matter carefully should such a situation arise again.

Softly, he said, "Who wants to control the situation now?"

It was a taunt, and if it didn't rouse her temper, it at least ruffled it a bit. She debated with herself silently, then said, "Maybe you're right. But so am I. The fact that physical attraction exists means very little unless emotions are involved as well. Maybe you can crawl into bed just because your body tells you to, but I can't."

After a moment, and in a very mild tone, he said, "I must say I'm encouraged."

"In what way?"

Gideon smiled. "I asked a very simple question, Maggie. I asked if you felt the same unusual reaction I felt."

Normally quick-witted, Maggie realized only then what she'd done. And she could only smile at herself for it. "I promptly went overboard with explanation, denial, and justification."

"You certainly did."

She sighed. "Don't gloat."

"I'll try not to, but it won't be easy. Will you answer the original question now, please?"

Maggie gave in with all the grace she could muster. "Yes, I felt something . . . unusual."

He nodded, his expression serious. "Good. We've established the fact that we both feel a special physical attraction for each other. Now we can work on the other levels."

"How are we going to do that?" she asked, wary but interested.

"The usual ways, I thought. Talk. Get to know each other. That sort of thing." Still wearing his serious expression and matter-of-fact voice, he added, "Mind you, there's nothing I'd rather do than climb into this absurd bed and let the other questions slide for the time being. But I do agree with you that those questions should be answered first."

She eyed him speculatively. "You do, do you?"

"Of course. I'm a mature man, after all. I'm hardly at the mercy of my hormones."

"Glad to hear it."

"So, we'll take things slow and easy." His voice had become brisk. "I'll sleep in the tent and bend my knees, shower and shave in cold water, and play the role of a stranger in a strange land."

"And I?"

"You will, I trust, be no more enigmatic than necessary so that I have at least a fair chance of finding the answers."

Maggie nodded slowly. "All right."

Gideon got to his feet. "Fine. See you in the morning."

She waited until he reached the door, then said, "Gideon? You forgot the blankets."

"No, I didn't. The temperature out there is in the high seventies. And my body temperature must be over a hundred. Good night, Maggie."

"Good night."

She stared at the closed door for a long time, then finally put her book on the table and blew out her lamp. She didn't get under the covers; the air temperature was comfortable, and like Gideon, she could tell that her own body temperature was way above normal. In fact, she felt feverish.

Lying back on her pillows in the dark caravan,

she replayed the past hours in her mind and tried to figure out what to do next. It would have been relatively simple without Gideon's presence; she'd just do as she had done before, listen and watch. But he was here now. Here, and bent on exploring a potential relationship. Every eye in the carnival—barring those of the few younger children—would be watching them either openly or covertly. And she doubted that Gideon would be out of her presence very often.

For the first time in her life she found herself torn between conflicting desires. She *wanted* to get to know Gideon, but at the same time she also wanted to find out who had killed Merlin and why. Involvement with Gideon meant she would have to be honest and her true self. Finding a killer required the opposite—detachment and deceitfulness.

Maggie wasn't accustomed to dividing herself. No matter how capricious and paradoxical she seemed to be, she was always working toward a single goal of some kind. But now . . . How could she show Gideon one face and the carnival another? How could she look for love and for a murderer at the same time?

Love?

Years before, Uncle Cyrus had told her that love would come when least expected, probably when least wanted, and undoubtedly at the most inconvenient time possible. As usual, he had been right. She didn't believe she was in love with Gideon, at least not yet, but for the first time in her life the possibility was definitely there. Her state now, feverish, restless, anxious, and undecided, was proof of that.

She was tempted to try to to find some excuse

to send Gideon away for a few weeks. If she told him the truth, he would certainly stay and quite likely insist on calling in the authorities as well. If she made up some other reason that he didn't believe or found impossible to accept, she could easily lose the opportunity to find out if there was more than a chance of love.

It wasn't in Maggie's nature to shirk responsibility; she had promised her family she would find Merlin's killer, and she intended to do just that. But she also intended to explore the possiblity of a relationship with Gideon. The problem, she thought, was how to accomplish both objectives simultaneously. It never occurred to her it was impossible, simply because "impossible" was a word stricken at an early age from her vocabulary. There was always a way to manage two things at once. The question was how to tackle her twin goals.

Until she could figure out some kind of workable game plan, she'd just have to play it by ear. A dangerous thing to do when you were looking for a killer.

Or looking for love.

The next morning, awakened at dawn by the sounds of hungry animals demanding breakfast, Gideon braved the cold water of the carnival's facilities. He ate breakfast with Maggie in her wagon and then went to be introduced to the other members of Wonderland's family.

Maggie had kept breakfast conversation casual, talking a great deal about the carnival and very little about herself. She seemed to Gideon to be in a peculiar mood—even for her. She was so vague and childlike that he couldn't for the life of him penetrate the veils of her enigmatic self. She was breaking her promise of the night before to be no more baffling than necessary. However, he didn't call her on it because he was far too interested in finding out why she had retreated from him.

In the meantime he played a waiting game, obediently accompanying her from person to person for an introduction. She gave each his name, added no explanatory comments, and no one seemed to expect more.

"Do they know who I am?" he asked after leaving Oswald's wagon. Oswald was the aristocratic gentleman who had worn a toga at the tea party; he was wearing the same costume today and had greeted the introduction with a fierce stare and an irritable, "Well, of course he is."

Maggie nodded, her expression utterly serene. "Naturally, they know you own the carnival now."

"Nobody's mentioned it," he observed.

"They know." She sent him a glance, then paused beside the tiger's cage, apparently to study the beast. Without looking at Gideon again she said mildly, "Oswald once taught at MIT. They called him another Einstein."

"Then what on earth is he doing here?"

"You've heard the expression 'future shock'?"

"Yes."

"It happened to Oswald, but a little differently. He could cope personally with how fast technology was advancing, but he saw further than anyone else. He didn't like what he saw. He told me once that we had too much knowledge and too little wisdom, that we were learning too fast. He said it terrified him."

After a moment Gideon said slowly, "So he just . . . retreated? Retired to an anachronism?"

"I suppose. Do you like Rajah?" She reached between the bars to scratch the tiger behind one lazy ear.

Gideon accepted the change of subject and looked at the drowsy tiger. "Beautiful. He seems tame enough."

Maggie began walking again toward another of the wagons. "Looks can be deceptive, especially with tigers." Her voice was bland. "There's muscle underneath the stripes. And a wide-awake predator behind the sleepy eyes."

Walking beside her, Gideon asked, "Is that a pointed reference?"

"That," she said, "was an observation." She stopped and reached out to knock lightly on the jamb of an open door. "Lamont," she called, "come out and meet Gideon."

A clown in full makeup—minus his red nose—immediately came out and sat down on the top step. He looked at Gideon, said, "Hi," in a distracted voice, and then looked mournfully at Maggie. It was something of a triumph that he could assume that expression, since a wide red smile was painted on his face.

"You should have a spare," she told him sternly.

"Well, I don't." Other than his makeup and a riotous wig of yellow hair, Lamont was wearing jeans and a T-shirt. He was, Gideon realized, hardly more than a kid. He reached up to finger his naked nose and gave Maggie another sad stare.

"I'll go into town sometime today," she told him, "and try to find another nose for you. All right?"

He nodded, still fingering his nose. "All right. Maybe you'll see Jasper there."

Maggie looked faintly surprised. "He's in town?"

"Well, sure. I mean, he must be, right?"

Gideon had the strangest impression that a silent message passed between the two of them, though there was no change of expression on either side.

After an instant Maggie nodded. "Beau's about to cast a shoe, Lamont. Maybe you'd better look at him."

"Okay. Nice meeting you," he added vaguely to Gideon, then scrambled off the steps and wandered away.

Maggie moved in the opposite direction toward a rather large tent pitched some yards away.

"What's Lamont's story?" Gideon asked her.

She glanced at him, a very faint crease between her brows. "Lamont? He's our blacksmith in addition to being a clown."

"I gathered that. I mean, why did he join the carnival?"

"Wonderland happened to be passing through his town a couple of years ago. He was sixteen, and he thought he'd better leave home."

"Why?"

She stopped and gazed up at him. "His father had some problems, and Lamont suffered for them."

"Abuse?" Gideon said slowly.

Maggie nodded. "It's funny about kids and clowns. Lamont never laughed very much as a kid, but now he paints on a smile and makes the kids laugh. He's still very insecure and anxious. That's why he worries about losing things."

"Why does he wear the makeup all the time?"

"Because he wants to. Maybe because he can't

quite smile without the paint. Not yet, anyway."
She began walking.

After a moment Gideon followed. He didn't much
like this. He wanted the carnival's future to be a
side issue between them, and Maggie was forcing
it center stage. He didn't resent the compassion
for these people that he was beginning to feel—
but he was aware of other feelings creeping in to
disturb him.

This place meant a lot to her, he could see that.
He couldn't help but wonder how much. Enough
so that Maggie was willing to make herself part of
a package deal? She was showing him these people as individuals, all of whom truly had nowhere
else they could fit in—but what if he ignored emotion and made the logical decision to sell? Would
her next ploy be to offer herself in exchange for an
assured future for the carnival?

How much of her enigmatic surface was the
chameleon face of an actress?

Gideon didn't want to think that. He didn't want
to believe that her passion had a price tag, that
her mystery was sheer artifice. But because he
had so many questions and so few answers, doubts
were nagging at him.

"Your world's beginning to look a little grim,"
he said.

"Not the world. This world is an escape from
grimness."

"What are you escaping from, Maggie?" He
needed answers of some kind.

"A boring summer vacation." A few feet from
the tent Maggie expertly balanced herself as a
raven-haired urchin about Sean's age erupted from
the opening and ran into her. "Where's the race,

Buster?" she asked calmly, setting him upright again.

He looked up at her with china-blue eyes shining angelic innocence. "I didn't do it, I swear I didn't."

"Do what?"

"Buster!"

The child closed one eye in a comical grimace as the enraged shout came from inside the tent. In a subdued tone he murmured, "I didn't forget to lay out papers for Alexander last night. He must have ate 'em. Or Sean stole 'em just to get me in trouble. Tell Ma I didn't forget, Maggie, please?" The stare he directed up at her was heartrending.

She didn't appear to be overly affected. "Buster, we made a deal, didn't we? I told you Alexander could sleep in your tent if your parents said he could, and if you trained him to use the papers."

"He don't like to use the papers," Buster said ingenuously. "He likes to use the floor of the tent. An' he's just a puppy, Maggie—"

Two more people emerged from the tent, an average-looking man somewhere in his thirties of medium build with a placid expression, and a strikingly beautiful woman whose fierce frown didn't quite hide her peculiarly vacant china-blue eyes. "Buster," she said, "get in here and clean up the mess!"

The boy looked up at Maggie's calm expression, glanced at Gideon's faintly amused one, then hung his head and turned back toward the tent. "Aw, Ma," he muttered, but quickened his pace when she said his name again warningly.

When he'd disappeared inside, Maggie said, "Sarah, Tom—this is Gideon."

Sarah looked him up and down with childlike curiosity. "What do you do?"

Having learned that carnies apparently didn't shake hands with strangers, Gideon left his in his pockets. "I'm a banker," he replied, wondering if that was what she was asking.

She looked at Maggie in bewilderment. "Are we trying to borrow money?"

"It hasn't come to that yet," Maggie answered.

Tom nodded a greeting to Gideon, then looked at his wife. "He owns us now. I told you," he said in a gentle voice.

Gideon wondered silently if he should point out that slavery was illegal. He decided not to.

"He looks different," Sarah said stubbornly.

"He was wearing a suit yesterday," Tom explained.

Sarah studied the visitor again. "You should stay away from suits," she told him. "They make you look mean."

"I'll remember that," Gideon said.

Dismissing him, she looked at Maggie. "Tom says Jasper went to town. Did he, Maggie?"

"I expect so."

"Of course he did," Tom said in the same gentle but firm voice. "He goes off on his own a lot, you know that." In a sudden tone of surprise he said, "Look at this. I've lost a button, Sarah." He was gazing down at his open hand, in which lay a button.

"You're so rough on shirts," his wife told him in a scolding voice. "I don't know what I'm going to do with you, Tom! Come inside and let me mend it."

Gideon, who had seen the other man unobtrusively and quite deliberately twist the button off, didn't say a word as he watched the couple retreat into their tent. He followed Maggie as she began moving toward another of the wagons. After several steps, and entirely unwilling, he said, "And them? Their story?"

"Buster was born in that tent," Maggie said. "Tom and Sarah joined when they were just kids. Together. Her family wanted to put her away."

"Insanity?"

Maggie stopped walking, gazing at the wagon still ahead of them. Then she looked up at him. "That's a relative term, isn't it? Sarah . . . couldn't cope. She got anxious, worried herself into hysterics without reason. Her family was embarrassed by her. And her problems were worsened by the fact that she's so beautiful. When she was fourteen, a strange man promised her a pretty necklace if she'd come with him. Tom protected her then, and he still does. He takes care of her. We all take care of her. She's safe here. And happy."

"What's their job in the carnival?"

"Tom runs a few games. Honest games. Sarah's our seamstress and designer. She makes beautiful costumes."

Gideon glanced around at the sprawl of wagons and tents and murmured almost to himself, "Sanctuary."

"You could say that."

He looked back at her serene face and bottomless, unreadable eyes. "You're arguing very persuasively for the defense," he told her a bit tautly.

"I'm just introducing you."

"We both know better. You're turning this into a personal matter. I can't make a dispassionate business decision as to whether I should sell after you've forced me to see these people as individuals." He was growing angry now, both because she had made him see what he would have liked to ignore, and because he wanted her to think about him rather than the damned carnival. He didn't like the doubts he was feeling.

"Is that the bottom line here? A purely business decision?" Her voice was still mild, but it had an edge now. "Because if that's so, the decision is already made. The logical, reasonable, *businesslike,* untroubling solution to your problem is simply to sell out. No hassles. No worries. No complications. And no need to get involved."

"And if I do? That puts paid to my chances with you, doesn't it, Maggie?"

She could feel her temper slipping from her control, and it was an alien sensation. She felt hot, tense, and even though a reasonable voice in her head was telling her why he was saying these things, it didn't help. A strange, shaken laugh escaped from her lips.

"Oh, am I the prize? If you're a good boy and do what I want you to do, then you'll get what *you* want? Is that the game we're playing here?"

"You tell me." His gray eyes were steely. "I'd really like to know, Maggie. You put a hell of a distance between us this morning, and since then you've talked about nothing except the carnival and these people. So I've got to wonder. Was that passion last night faked? Are you the bait to keep Wonderland in business?"

She took a step back, almost as if he had hit her. In a soft, shaking voice she said, "You want to sell the carnival? Fine. I'll buy it. Right down to the broken wagon wheel the birds roost on. Tell your lawyer to get in touch."

Gideon knew he'd gone too far. "Maggie—"

"Leave. Now. Your *business* here is concluded."
She turned on her heel and walked away.

He stared after her, a strange tightness in his
chest. "Damn," he muttered.

Tina found Maggie brushing one of the horses a
few minutes later and stood watching the rhyth-
mic strokes. She looked at the younger woman's
set face, then said, "He's gone. Got in his car and
left."

"I know."

Lifting herself up to sit on a feed barrel, Tina
said, "So?"

Maggie turned away from the horse and sighed.
She dropped the brush into a wooden box holding
several of them, then sat down on an overturned
water bucket. "So what?"

Tina grimaced faintly. "Hey, this is me, remember? I gave you a reading when you first got here.
Can't hide from Madame Valentina." She smiled,
then sobered. "We both know you're a very smart
lady. And you're doing a damn good job of holding
this place together. Old Balthazar never did so
well. But you don't belong here any more than
that redheaded devil who just roared out of here
does."

"I fit in here," Maggie said, knowing it was true.

"Sure you do. But you don't belong. The rest of
us are all varying degrees of crazy; you're a little
strange, that's all."

"Thanks a lot."

Tina smiled again. "My point is that you shouldn't
wreck your chances with Gideon because of us. In
your life, we're temporary; he looks like being
long-term."

Maggie was silent for a moment, then said, "You all heard, didn't you?"

"Malcolm heard, since you were so near his wagon. Telephone, telegraph, tell Malcolm. Everybody knows you and Gideon had an argument. Lot of speculation going on."

"I lost my temper, Tina. I've never done that before. And it was stupid. It was inevitable that he'd have doubts, that he'd think I was . . . Damn." She shook her head slightly. "I don't know if he'll come back."

"He will."

"Been looking into your crystal ball?" Maggie kept her voice light.

"No. I saw his face before he got into his car. He wasn't angry. He looked like a man who'd been punched in the stomach—and hadn't been very happy to find out it was his own fist that did the job."

Maggie drew a shaky breath. "It was a logical question he asked—if I was bait to keep the carnival intact. The worst of it is that I *did* think about it when we first met. You know, if I could distract him. But I couldn't go through with it."

"Not magnanimous enough?" Tina asked with a grin.

The answering grin was a little strained. "Not dispassionate enough."

"Oh. It's like that, huh?"

"In spades. As much as I've grown to love this place and you people, Gideon wouldn't have to offer anything in return. Hell, he wouldn't even have to say please."

"Does he know that?"

"Obviously not. I did too good a job of holding him at a distance today. And then I got really stupid and started telling him a little about the people here. He probably started to wonder if I'd decided to try *compassion* first."

"Ouch," Tina murmured.

"Yeah. The thing is, I know without a shadow of a doubt that if I *did* tell him he could have me if he spared the carnival, he'd walk away. He's not a man to buy a woman—no matter what the price tag reads. What's between us is separate from the carnival, but I think he began doubting that I felt that way."

"Maybe you better clear that up when he comes back," Tina suggested dryly.

They had grown to be friends in the past weeks, but Maggie hadn't dared confide her real reason for joining the carnival. So she worded her response to that carefully. "I'll try. But the fate of the carnival is in his hands, and he's going to have a hard time forgetting that."

"So you were bluffing when you said you'd buy it?" Tina's voice was casual.

Maggie swore inwardly; she'd hoped that little item had gone unheard. It wouldn't do for anyone here to find out she could afford to buy the carnival. "No. I'd raise the money somehow. I won't let Wonderland be scrapped, Tina. Tell everyone else, okay?" There was nothing else she could say.

"I'll pass the word." Tina tilted her head and studied the younger woman thoughtfully. "I guess I can see what you're getting at, though. This place isn't Barnum and Bailey, but the price tag for the whole shebang wouldn't be peanuts; raising the money to buy it would put you in hock up to your ears. Better if you can persuade Gideon just to leave us alone."

"Right."

"It is a problem between you two, though. How're you going to convince him you and the carnival aren't a package deal?"

"I don't know," Maggie said. "All I can do is tell him. Whether he believes it is up to him."

"Guess you're right."

Maggie shook her head. "Well, we'll see. By the way, what's this about Jasper?"

"Nobody's seen him since last night."

Conscious of a faint chill, Maggie kept her voice casual and puzzled. "The stuff about his being in town—?"

"A story for Gideon. He might have—overreacted to the news of one of us coming up missing." Tina shrugged a little. "You weren't here when Merlin disappeared, but I told you how it was. The police didn't give a damn until he was found dead, and then they were all over us. Everybody's paranoid, I think, worried that it could happen again."

"Do you think something's happened to him?"

"Who knows?" Tina's voice was helpless rather than heartless. "He *does* go off on his own sometimes, but it's usually just a few hours. If he isn't back by dark . . ."

Maggie nodded and after a moment said dryly, "Tell everyone to stop innocently remarking on it, all right? Gideon picked up on the undercurrent when Lamont mentioned it, and I think he saw Tom distract Sarah by pulling a button off his shirt. Gideon's hardly an idiot."

"Umm. Gotcha. Has he figured out you're not exactly one either?"

"Like you, he thinks I'm strange."

Tina dropped off the barrel and grinned. "But fascinating," she added.

Maggie sighed. "I'm getting a little tired of being fascinating, friend. It's like having a big chest; men stare at it so much they never see your face."

"I wouldn't know about that," Tina said with a mournful glance down at herself.

Maggie laughed and watched her friend saunter away. The spurt of humor faded, leaving her in a mood that was totally unfamiliar to her. Knowing herself thoroughly was the constant that enabled her to keep her balance no matter what lunacy was going on all around her; that easy self-knowledge seemed to be slipping away from her now. Unlike Gideon, Maggie rarely tried to impose control on any situation; her method was far more simple and a great deal more risky.

Presented with the unknown or unfamiliar, she merely immersed herself in it. Detached and observant, she stood in the middle of chaos and waited patiently for it to make sense to her. A true chameleon, she let her colors change to match her surroundings by sheer instinct, responding to people as they expected or required her to respond.

But with Gideon, the instincts themselves were chaotic. He said he wanted her to be herself, and that was a requirement never asked of her before. She knew who she was. What she was. The problem was that her instinct was to be what *Gideon* expected her to be—and he wasn't even sure what that was. As his idea of her changed, she instantly and unconsciously changed as well.

No wonder the man was baffled.

And no wonder, she thought, that her emotions and instincts were short-circuiting all over the place. What he thought of her at any given moment was so clearly evident to her that she responded spontaneously. He had thought her child-like and vague at their first meeting; she had donned those colors automatically. He had thought himself in the middle of an asylum; she had allowed a little madness to show itself. He had looked at her with a man's desire; she had felt the jarring awareness of her body as a woman's. He had expected her to hold him at a distance this morning after the interlude in her wagon last night, and she had. And when he had taunted her in anger, she had lost her temper *despite the fact that she had expected him to do just that.*

It was all her. Everything he had seen in her *was* her. But he wasn't seeing her as a whole, integrated personality, and because of that it was literally impossible for her to present herself to him the way he asked.

"Strange nothing," Maggie muttered to herself. "I'm as crazy as the rest of them."

Uncle Cyrus had told her the peculiar ability was her strength. He had also said that even though most people would look no further than their own idea of what she was—or was supposed to be—one day someone would want to look much deeper, to reach through the reflective surface and see what was there. The duration, he'd warned, would be bothersome.

Uncle Cyrus was sometimes prone to understatement.

Still, it was rather reassuring, she thought, that Uncle Cyrus was always right. He'd said that she would feel disjointed and confused for a bit, but then would regain her balance. There would come a point—a sudden one, he was willing to bet—when that other person's idea of her would clash head-on with some bedrock part of herself, and she would begin reacting *for* herself, reflecting what she truly was. She wouldn't entirely lose her chameleon colors . . . but for that other person from that point on, there would never be any doubt as to who and what she was.

Maggie didn't know if Gideon was that person, although it certainly looked that way. She rose and began making her way toward her wagon, trying to stop thinking about it. About him. Because, she knew, Tina could easily be wrong. He might not return. She didn't like the way the possibility made her feel. She didn't like feeling it at all.

The morning dragged on—still with no sign of Jasper—and afternoon came. Maggie was kneeling at the edge of the woods potting a wild rose bush that Sean had dug up for her as a present when she heard the car. She sat back on her heels and brushed her hands together as she watched Gideon get out of his car, look around briefly, and then come toward her.

He was carrying a small package wrapped colorfully and sporting a cheerful bow, and his expression was very sober. He kept his eyes fixed on her, ignoring the interested stares coming from several points in the encampment. When he reached her, he knelt down and looked at her steadily.

Maggie glanced at the package, which he had set on the ground, then met his gaze.

"A peace offering," he said quietly.

"What is it?" Her tone matched his.

A crooked smile softened his hard face. "A tasteful selection of noses for Lamont. There was a novelty shop in town."

It was unusual. Unexpected. Maybe even a little bit mad. Maggie felt her own lips curving in a smile. "Lamont will be delighted," she murmured.

"I bought a tent too," Gideon said. "A little bigger, so I won't have to bend my knees. And a fancy collar for Leo, in case Tina hasn't gotten around to making him one."

"It sounds like you're planning to stick around," she said in a neutral tone.

"I want to. If you'll let me." He reached out to touch her cheek very lightly with the tips of his fingers, and his expression suddenly held something fierce. "I'm sorry, Maggie."

Take care of the sense,
and the sounds will take care of themselves.

Four

After a moment Maggie drew back just enough so that his hand fell away from her. "Maybe you are. But you're still not sure about my motives. I can tell you that our relationship is quite separate from the fate of the carnival; I can tell you that whatever you decide won't influence my personal feelings, but I can't make you believe it. I could buy Wonderland from you, but that wouldn't be easy for me, and I consider it a last resort."

Gideon looked at her steadily. "All right. Let's solve that problem right now. I don't want Wonderland. I don't need the problems of owning it, or the proceeds from selling it. So as soon as I get probate, I'll deed it over to someone else. Anyone in the carnival except you." He smiled. "I don't want to be accused of trying to buy something that isn't for sale."

Slowly, she said, "I suppose we could form a co-op. Let everyone have a share."

He opened his mouth, then shut it quickly.

Maggie had to smile. "I know. Then the lunatics

really will be running the asylum. But they're a family, and they take care of each other. Tina could handle the business end; she's the shrewdest."

"What about you?" Gideon asked.

"I'm temporary. In the fall I'll go back to school."

His eyes narrowed. "Then this isn't your life. Your world."

Maggie dropped her gaze to the rosebush, idly picking off a few damaged leaves. "My world is wherever I am."

"That's no answer."

Her instinct was to be vague because he expected her to be, but she fought against herself; if he was going to see her clearly, she would at least have to try to meet him halfway. It was surprisingly difficult. "You're wrong," she said. "That's the most important answer of all. It's why I fit in here so well, even though I wasn't born carny and never saw this place until a few weeks ago."

Gideon watched her intently, fascinated by what he was seeing. Her face was serene, her eyes limpid, and yet her tone of voice was one he'd never heard before, soft and firm without being at all childlike or ambiguous. He didn't understand the contrast. "Where were you born?"

"In Virginia. An only child of two extremely practical and logical people. They didn't quite know what to make of me. Mother still doesn't. Dad was killed ten years ago."

"I'm sorry. An accident?"

She smiled suddenly, and Gideon felt his heart stop. There it was, that fey smile that was peculiarly wise and tolerant and a little bit mad, as if she knew secret things the rest of the world hadn't begun to discover.

"You could say that. My wonderfully practical

and logical parent decided to take up hang glid-ing. He wasn't very good at it, I'm afraid. But he did enjoy himself, even Mother admitted that. And to be killed while you're having fun isn't the worst way to go."

Gideon decided not to ask. "You—have a unique way of looking at things."

She sent him a glance that was a bit mischie-vous. "Not so unique in my family."

"I thought you said your mother didn't under-stand you."

"No, but then, Mother's the unusual one among all my relatives. The rest . . . Well, put it this way. If I owned Wonderland and they found out, every-one would want to join."

"You're kidding."

"Not at all. To say that my family is eccentric would be a considerable understatement."

"What am I getting myself into?"

"Oh, you don't have to worry. We don't see much of each other, really. The usual family gatherings is all. Other people seem to get nervous when we're all together." She looked at him again, tran-quil innocence in her face. "I can't imagine why."

"The hell you can't." This time, Gideon felt on reasonably solid ground. "I may not have figured you out completely, but one thing I do know is that you're a long way from dumb."

Maggie smiled slightly, but didn't comment. "The point I wanted to make is that even though I wasn't born carny, this *is* my world. I made it mine when I came here. And I'm quite comfort-able here. I don't like being logical and practical; it's so uninteresting."

"So you go a little mad whenever you're sur-rounded by lunatics?"

She chuckled softly. "You are worried about that, aren't you?"

He had the grace to look a bit sheepish. "If you mean I need to be reassured as to the state of your sanity—you're right. Just tell me you aren't dangerously insane."

"Well, if I were, I'd hardly admit it, would I?"

"Maggie."

She sighed. "Gideon, I hold three university degrees. I've earned a grandmaster rating at chess, a gourmet rating as a cook, and I'm licensed to fly a small plane—though I have been known to buzz people on the ground. When I was nineteen, I climbed Mount Everest; at twenty I sailed the South China Sea in a very small boat; and at twenty-one I participated in a hot-air-balloon race across Europe—which I won.

"I talk to plants and animals. I generally know why people do or say the things they do even if they don't know why. I'm great with crossword puzzles, trivia on most subjects, and, with only a bobby pin or a rubber band I can fix just about any machine. I hate cheating in any form, short-cuts that miss great scenery, the designated hitter, and asparagus." Shrugging, she finished, "Among my family and in my world, none of that makes me unusual. What does it make me in your world?"

Softly, he said, "Exceptional."

Maggie shook her head and said, "But does it make me sane? You can't prove sanity, not really. We all believe we're sane—or hope so. All I can tell you is that I've never had a problem functioning in your world or mine; no one's ever threatened to lock me up; and that I believe I'm no more insane than the average person. And that will have to be good enough."

"It is. More than enough."

"I'm glad to hear it. How about you?"

"What about me?"

She gave him a solemn look. "From my point of view, you know, you aren't exactly the norm."

"I always thought I was sane. Since yesterday, I'm not so sure."

"What happened yesterday?"

Gideon shook his head, smiling. "I refuse to answer that on the grounds that it might later be used against me. Speaking of which, why are we on the ground?"

"I am on the ground because Sean decided to uproot a pretty rosebush for me, and I'm potting it in this old water bucket. You're on the ground because it's difficult to talk to someone who's sitting at your feet."

"Concisely explained. At the risk of sounding less than manly, I'm getting a cramp in my calf."

Maggie lifted an eyebrow at him. "Men don't get cramps?"

"Only after marathons or strenuous gym workouts; it's considered wimpy to get one simply by kneeling on the ground. Can we get up now?"

"We probably should. The natives are getting restless."

Gideon glanced toward the wagons and tents and encountered a number of curious stares. "True. I forgot about them."

"They didn't forget about you—ouch!"

He looked at her, then quickly reached out to take her hand. "Here, let me."

"It's just a thorn—"

"I know. Hold still."

Maggie did, allowing him to gently extract the thorn from her index finger. As she gazed at his bent head she began to feel curiously breathless. Despite being the center of all eyes, they seemed to be alone, isolated. Sunlight filtered by the trees wove a pattern of light and shadow over them, and a warm breeze whispered as it touched the grass and trees. And them.

All of Maggie's senses came vividly alive in a way she'd never known before. Her sight and hearing were acute, and the feeling of his cool hands touching hers was so intense it felt almost shatteringly intimate. And then he lifted her hand, his lips closing over her index finger, and she felt a totally alien explosion of heat somewhere deep inside her.

Her thoughts scattered like autumn leaves, fluttering unconnected through her mind. He shouldn't be doing this, her hands were dirty . . . he had a cramp in his leg . . . and people were watching . . . why did she suddenly feel naked?

"Don't," she murmured huskily.

Gideon raised his head, looking at her with darkened eyes. A muscle flexed in his jaw, and his hands were still holding hers, caressing it. His strong features held the stamp of that fierce thing she had seen before and heard in his voice, that unconsciously relentless . . . need? Determination? Whatever it was, it triggered instincts far deeper and more complex than those of a chameleon.

"Don't what?" His voice was soft, uneven.

She couldn't look away, couldn't reclaim her hand. His eyes were like storms in his taut face, holding a violence of emotion contained only by fragile barriers. She couldn't answer his question aloud, but she thought he must have found some kind of answer in her face.

"Maggie," he whispered, and bent his head again, pressing his lips into her palm.

It was as if some softly playing music inside Maggie suddenly reached a crescendo, a tense, breathless moment when her heart thudded wildly. Her response to him was physical, emotional, on every level of herself; she had never in her life been so completely attuned to another human being.

The strength of that feeling was brief, reaching a peak and then ebbing slowly until it was only a pulsing warmth inside her, but it left behind it a confused excitement that made her retreat cautiously, as if from the edge of something not quite stable. Very gently, she withdrew her hand from his grasp.

"I thought I'd put the rosebush beside my steps," she said conversationally, looking at the shrub in question. "It'll probably bloom at least once more before fall."

"I'm getting there, Maggie." His voice was still roughly uneven, low. "I'm finding the answers. You can pull away now, but what happens when there aren't any more questions? How will you pull away from me then?"

"Maybe that's the last question." She rose to her feet, watching as he did as well. "Maybe by then—we'll both know the answer."

Gideon looked at her for a moment, not angry but intent, searching. Then he bent to pick up his gift for Lamont and Maggie's potted rosebush. Straightening, he said, "I've always considered myself a patient man. We'll find out, won't we?"

They began walking toward Maggie's wagon, and she felt a dim spurt of amusement at the way everyone immediately became very busy, very active; until then, they'd all resembled waxworks figures. Gideon had noticed as well.

"I suppose we should tell everyone about the carnival's future, before they explode from curiosity," he said dryly.

"It might be best," she agreed.

Gideon looked down at her. "Who's Jasper?"

His voice had been casual, but Maggie knew he had been alerted that something was going on. She kept her own voice matter-of-fact. "Three of us take care of the animals—Farley, Jasper, and me. Jasper's been with Wonderland since the beginning. He's great with the animals."

"So where is he?"

"He goes off on his own sometimes. Probably in town now. I expect he'll turn up before dark." She hoped he would. She really hoped he would.

"And if he doesn't?"

They had reached her wagon. Gideon set the rosebush down beside the steps and then straightened, looking at her as he waited for her response.

She hesitated, then said, "Wonderland seems to be perpetual, but the people change. It isn't unusual to find one carny more or less from one day to the next. To some people, the carnival is a stopover for days. Or years." Something in what she'd said rang a bell in her mind. She had overlooked something, hadn't considered a possibility that should have been obvious. And something Gideon had said earlier . . .

Sanctuary.

"What are you telling me?" Gideon asked bluntly, frowning a bit.

Maggie forced herself to keep her mind on what she was saying. "I'm telling you that we don't ask a lot of questions here. If somebody goes away, we assume he wanted to."

"You don't expect him to come back, do you?"

"I hope he does."

After a moment Gideon appeared to accept that. He nodded and said, "Why don't we take the noses to Lamont, and then you can finish introducing me."

The carnies took the news of their future cooperative ownership of Wonderland with their usual aplomb: an argument broke out as to whether there should be equal or differing shares. Maggie made no effort to settle the dispute, merely leaving them to it and telling Gideon she'd help him pitch his new tent if he liked. She took down the old tent while he got the new one out of his car, and they worked together.

"Do you really think a co-op is a good idea?" he asked her, driving a stake into the ground.

Sorting through the tent poles, she said absently, "Of course it is. Don't worry—they'll work everything out."

"You know them better than I do." Gideon sat back on his heels as he looked at her, wondering again just exactly what it was that she was hiding from him. There was something going on, he knew that. It was partly Jasper's disappearance, but he'd felt the undercurrents before that.

Outsider or not, Maggie understood these people, but to him they were maddeningly elusive. However unusual or absurd this place seemed to be on the surface, there was an underlying tension that made him apprehensive. He had assumed at first it was because he held the carnival's fate in his hands, so the anxiety the others felt about their future had touched him. Despite his announcement about the decision he and Maggie had reached, the level of strain was still high. He had a feeling that was why everyone was arguing now, and he thought Maggie knew it as well.

"Leo likes his collar," she noted, still in the absent tone he was beginning to believe hid something she didn't want him to understand.

Gideon glanced toward the steps of her wagon, where the peculiar-looking cat sprawled with his chin raised and a ridiculous Cheshire-cat grin on his face. Around his mottled-brown neck was a fancy red collar complete with rhinestones and a dangling silver tag that proclaimed his name and where he belonged. His dubious attitude toward Gideon had vanished the instant the collar had been buckled around his neck, and he had since shown a fawning tendency to remain near his new idol.

"That cat is . . ." Gideon's voice trailed off.

"Hard to define, isn't he? I can't fasten these lines until the stakes are in."

Turning his gaze somewhat balefully to the canvas spread out on the ground, Gideon said, "This is not exactly my idea of a courtship."

Maggie watched him finish driving the stakes into the ground, deciding not to question his choice of nouns. "I must admit, I'm a little surprised myself. Do investment bankers usually vacation in tents? Or is this a vacation?"

"It is now. While I was in town today, I called the bank and took a leave of absence. As for the tent, I haven't heard a better offer."

Ignoring his remark, she asked curiously, "Tell me something. Do you always abandon your job and preferred lifestyle when you meet a woman you're interested in?"

"No, I usually just send flowers." Gideon tossed the mallet aside, regarding her with a wry expression. "If the response is favorable, after that usually comes dinner and maybe the theater. Conversation. Normal stuff."

"You could always wait until fall," she said. "I'll be back in Richmond then. Plenty of restaurants and theaters there. And florists."

He looked at her thoughtfully. "Do you happen to be aware of the fact that I live in San Francisco?"

"Balthazar's attorney mentioned it."

"That puts three thousand miles between my home and your home base."

"Nasty commute," she observed. "But we don't need to worry about that now, do we? Or are your intentions totally honorable?"

"My intentions," Gideon said, "include figuring you out and getting this damned tent up. I haven't thought beyond that."

"Haven't you?"

He wished her eyes weren't green. It was unfair for any woman to have eyes like that. "Dammit, Maggie, you know what I want. I want to be your lover."

A small voice suddenly piped up, "What's a lover? An' you've got the lines all tangled."

Maggie got to her feet, saying easily, "Sean knows all about tents, don't you, Sean?"

"Course I do," the boy said scornfully.

"Then you can help Gideon." She looked from the boy to the man—who didn't appear exactly thrilled by his prospective helper. Hiding her amusement, she said, "I think they've argued over there long enough. I should get things settled down."

"Sure," Gideon said, wondering what on earth had possessed him to think he could conduct any kind of courtship in the middle of a lunatic carnival. He watched Maggie stroll off toward the fractious group on the other side of the encampment, wishing she wore clothes a little less threatening to his blood pressure. Today, she was wearing jeans and some kind of a halter top, her long hair hanging down her back in a single braid. From certain angles she looked about sixteen; from other angles, she definitely didn't.

"What's a lover?" Sean persisted.

Gideon looked at the boy and sighed. "Someone who loves," he said, and only then heard what he was saying. Somewhat hastily, he added, "You're the tent expert, Sean, so show me how it's done."

Maggie settled the argument simply by reminding everyone that it would be months before a final decision would have to be made, and that they had plenty of time to work out a fair division of shares. As the group broke up, she walked with Tina back toward the older woman's wagon.

"Told you he'd be back," Tina murmured. "That little scene between you two looked pretty intense."

"It felt that way too."

"So why's he with my son right now instead of you?"

"Don't rush me, Tina. Isn't a woman allowed a little time to make up her mind?"

"Sure. But you've already made up your mind."

"Well, a little time to make up *his* mind, then.

I'm not really in the market for a scrapbook full of memories."

"Like I said, he looks like being long-term to me."

Maggie smiled a little, but said, "We'll see. Anyway, since he's going to deed the carnival over, the lawyers will need a complete accounting for all the paperwork. Didn't I leave the books in your wagon last week?"

"Yeah, on the shelf above my bed. You go ahead. I promised Lamont I'd watch him model his new noses."

Leaving her friend, Maggie went on to the wagon, finding the carnival's account books easily enough. She debated returning the books to her own wagon, but decided against it. Sitting down on Tina's bed, she tore a blank page from the most recent account book, found a pencil on the bedside table, and began going through the oldest accounts.

She had looked over the accounts before, but without any specific purpose; this time, she had one. With so little to go on in the matter of her cousin's death, Maggie had been more or less hamstrung. She had watched and listened, getting to know the individuals of the carnival, but that hadn't helped. As far as she'd been able to determine, Merlin had made no enemies and had been well liked. In fact, he had been a very nice old man, almost impossible to anger and quite kind to others.

Since she hadn't found a clue as to *who* would have killed him, she had turned her attention to the question of why. And there again she'd been stymied. What possible reason would anyone have for killing a sweet old man? If she'd been given to doubting her Aunt Julia's pronouncements, she would have begun believing the police's verdict of accidental death, but Maggie had known her aunt too long to consider that.

It was only when Gideon's remark about Wonderland's being a sanctuary had connected with her own words about the place's being a stopover for some people that a possible motive had occurred to her. A sanctuary was a safe place; in historical times even criminals had taken advantage of that fact.

So what if, she asked herself, one of the people here had something to hide—and to protect? A dangerous secret, maybe? Merlin could have found out somehow, and he'd been, above all else, an honest and scrupulous man; he might well have threatened to expose his killer. He certainly wouldn't have been the first man murdered to protect a secret.

Which left Maggie with a very big question.

The account books of Wonderland were so stuffed with details they were beautifully complete—and absolutely chaotic. From its beginnings more than thirty years before to the present, every aspect of the carnival had been written down. The acquisition, birth, or death of every animal; totals from gate receipts, food bills, supplies, repairs, and equipment; yearly inventories of all equipment, livestock, and so on.

There was also a complete record of every stop Wonderland had made in its journeys, noted by date and place, as well as dated notations of the arrival and departure of every carny who had ever been a part of the carnival.

Those notations interested Maggie. She needed to narrow her list of suspects, and arbitrarily she decided to look no further back than seven years—simply because of the statute of limitations. She reasoned that Merlin would have had to have *found* some evidence of dishonesty, something concrete, and to Maggie's mind that indicated the possibility of robbery.

It made sense to her. If someone had committed a robbery of some kind and needed to lie low until the statute of limitations had expired, what better place than a carnival? They were almost always on the move, traveling back roads and staying only briefly in towns, mostly small towns at that.

She knew these people well by now, and she knew that none of them was a cold-blooded killer. But she was less sure that several wouldn't kill to protect themselves or some secret wealth. This was a perfect place to hide—and to hide something valuable; unless they were unusually bulky, any number of items could be hidden away in the big, ornate antique wagons.

It was a long shot, and Maggie knew it. But she was running out of time. The carnies themselves didn't believe Merlin's death had been an accident, and an unsolved murder was far harder on the innocent than the guilty; they were all tense and jumpy. Now Jasper had vanished, and Maggie had a hollow feeling he wouldn't be coming back.

She wasn't yet ready to confide in Gideon, because she was certain he would insist they call the police. And though Maggie doubted the police would be interested without some kind of evidence, the killer undoubtedly would.

So all she had to go on a few minutes later as she closed the account books and replaced them on the shelf was a list containing only two names. Beside the names of the two most recent additions to Wonderland, she had noted down the date and location of the carnival at those times.

Lamont had joined three years ago while Wonderland had been in Texas; specifically, some miles outside Dallas.

Farley had joined four years ago when the carnival passed through Little Rock, Arkansas.

After staring at her notes for a moment, Maggie folded up the page and tucked it into her pocket. Now came the hard part. Somehow, she had to find out what currently unsolved robberies had been committed in the right areas during those two periods.

Great.

There were a number of problems. Access to information, for one. Uncle Cyrus could find out what she needed to know, and he was probably the only one who could—if she could get word to him, that is. Gideon was, as he'd been from the beginning, another of the problems. She couldn't hold him off much longer when it wasn't what she wanted to do, and she had the unnerving feeling that it would be pretty much impossible to hide anything from him once he was in her bed.

They were sitting on a powder keg here. There was a killer among them, everyone was unusually tense and secretive, and Jasper had come up missing.

Jasper . . . where did he fit in? Maggie wondered. Another victim who had accidently found something he shouldn't have? He'd been with Wonderland for more than twenty years. Did that mean anything? She had checked his wagon earlier, discovering that all his belongings were accounted for; there was no indication that he'd decided to leave on his own. And though he'd often wandered off, he'd been gone too long this time.

Far too long.

"Are you still here?" Tina came into her wagon, looking faintly surprised. "A problem with the books?"

"No, I was just . . . thinking. Where's Gideon?"

"Looking for you. Having a hard time too. Everyone keeps asking him how we should portion out shares, and he's obviously not about to offer an opinion."

"Smart man. Any sign of Jasper yet?"

"Nothing. Tom and Farley combed the woods a little while ago, but they didn't find anything. It's getting late too. Malcolm has the tea party going."

"You aren't playing?"

"Not today. You'd better go rescue that man of yours. He was looking tense when I last saw him."

Taking that advice to heart, Maggie left Tina's wagon and went in search of Gideon. She found him leaning against a wagon wheel as he watched the ritual poker game from a distance of several yards, his expression far less bemused today than it had been yesterday.

"Didn't they invite you to play?" Maggie asked him.

"Yes. Maggie, where have you been?"

"Making sure we had all the paperwork your lawyers will need for the transfer of ownership."

"This place has paperwork?" he asked incredulously.

"You'd be surprised," she murmured.

"I am. I'm also trying to think of a way to get even with you for leaving me in the hands of that . . . that demon seed."

"Sean?" Maggie smiled up at him. "He couldn't have been all that bad."

"I'll admit I'm not used to children. But Sean is not a child. A midget, maybe. Do you realize he hears and sees everything? I mean everything. He started telling me things I really didn't want to know."

"For instance?"

"Tina colors her hair. Oswald is trying to teach his parrot to say some . . . impolite things. Farley wears blue shorts under his kilt—which answers *that* age-old question. And somebody named Merlin found a bear pond. What on earth is a bear pond, and who the hell is Merlin?"

"A bear pond? Beats me. And Merlin was before my time. Gideon, I should go into town so I can call my mother; I promised her I'd keep in touch. Do you want to get away for a while? Have dinner or something?"

"I thought you'd never ask."

Maggie smiled. "All right. I'll change and meet you by your car in a few minutes."

She left word with Tina and then changed into a silky skirt and print blouse. Within half an hour she and Gideon were on their way into town. Conversation was casual, with Maggie setting the tone by asking him about his work and his usual lifestyle. He answered her questions as lightly as they were asked, feeling a definite relief to be away from the carnival.

When they reached the small town, Gideon rather dryly suggested the only restaurant that wasn't part of a fast-food chain; it had a lounge that served drinks and provided piano music, and the food was supposed to be the best in town.

"I guess that means more variety than burgers and fries?" Maggie said with a laugh.

"Probably. Are you game?"

"Sure. Look, there's a phone out front. Why don't you go in and get us a table while I make my call?"

"All right. But don't let some stranger steal you away."

"I'm not in the mood to be stolen."

"I hope you're in the mood to dance."

Maggie waited until they got out of the car to answer, then said, "I love dancing. Meet you inside."

She went to the pay phone on the corner, just down the street from the building. She glanced over her shoulder to see that Gideon had gone inside. Before she could even lift the receiver, a somewhat imposing and very familiar figure came around the corner of the building and smiled at her.

"Uncle Cyrus! What are you doing here?"

The moment he was inside the restaurant, Gideon knew that they'd have no trouble getting a table; the place was only about half full. Still he reserved a table for seven o'clock and said they'd be in the lounge until then. He returned to the door to wait for Maggie, looking out through the glass panes more to reassure himself that she was still there than out of curiosity about her call.

She wasn't alone.

The man standing before her, head bent as he listened to her talk, looked like a king-size version of a Kentucky colonel. He was a big man, dressed all in white and leaning slightly on a gold-headed cane. From where Gideon stood, the man looked very old; he had thick white hair and a full white beard. But there was something about him that spoke of a great deal of physical strength no matter how many years he had put behind him.

Gideon watched as Maggie talked earnestly, then saw her pull a folded piece of paper from her skirt pocket and hand it to the man. The paper was unfolded and studied, and then the man said something to her that brought a smile to her face.

Gideon retreated from the door, feeling curiously unsettled. What the hell was going on here?

*It looked good-natured, she thought,
still, it had very long claws
and a great many teeth,
so she felt it ought to be
treated with respect.*

Five

Gideon said nothing about what he'd seen. At first. When Maggie came inside the restaurant, her eyes were as guileless as a child's. They went into the dimly lighted lounge where a bored-looking young man in a dinner jacket was playing the piano. There were only about a dozen people, couples mostly, and everyone was talking in hushed tones.

They found a small table tucked away in a corner, and when the waitress came, Gideon ordered brandy; he thought he might need it. Maggie ordered plain tomato juice.

"I get strange when I drink," she explained.

Gideon waited until the waitress had left, then said, "You get strange when you drink?"

"All right, then—I get even stranger. What's wrong, Gideon?"

As usual in her company, he found it all too unnervingly easy to say exactly what was on his mind. "You tell me. What's going on?"

Her candid green eyes studied him for a moment, and also as usual, she surprised him.

OPEN YOUR HEART TO LOVE. YOU'LL BE LOVESWEPT WITH THIS FREE OFFER.

HERE'S WHAT YOU GET:

1. **FREE!** SIX NEW LOVESWEPT NOVELS! You get 6 beautiful stories filled with passion, romance, laughter, and tears...exciting romances to stir the excitement of falling in love... again and again.

2. **FREE!** A BEAUTIFUL MAKEUP CASE WITH A MIRROR THAT LIGHTS UP! What could be more useful than a makeup case with a mirror that lights up*? Once you open the tortoise-shell finish case, you have a choice of brushes... for your lips, your eyes, and your blushing cheeks.

*(batteries not included)

3. **SAVE!** MONEY-SAVING HOME DELIVERY! Join the Loveswept at-home reader service and we'll send you 6 new novels each month. You always get 15 days to preview them before you decide. Each book is yours for only $2.09 — a savings of 41¢ per book.

4. BEAT THE CROWDS! You'll always receive your Loveswept books before they are available in bookstores. You'll be the first to thrill to these exciting new stories.

BE LOVESWEPT TODAY — JUST COMPLETE, DETACH AND MAIL YOUR FREE-OFFER CARD.

FREE – LIGHTED MAKEUP CASE!
FREE – 6 LOVESWEPT NOVELS!

- NO OBLIGATION
- NO PURCHASE NECESSARY

(DETACH AND MAIL CARD TODAY.)

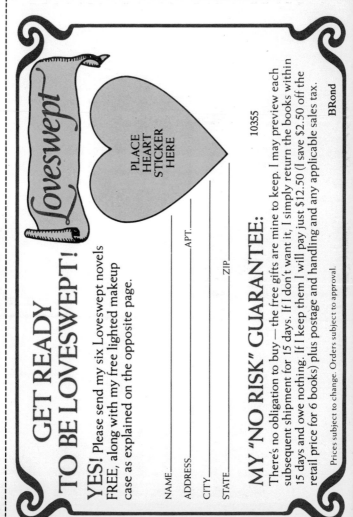

GET READY TO BE LOVESWEPT!

YES! Please send my six Loveswept novels FREE, along with my free lighted makeup case as explained on the opposite page.

PLACE HEART STICKER HERE

NAME _____

ADDRESS _____ APT. _____

CITY _____

STATE _____ ZIP _____

10355

MY "NO RISK" GUARANTEE:

There's no obligation to buy — the free gifts are mine to keep. I may preview each subsequent shipment for 15 days. If I don't want it, I simply return the books within 15 days and owe nothing. If I keep them I will pay just $12.50 (I save $2.50 off the retail price for 6 books) plus postage and handling and any applicable sales tax.

BRond

Prices subject to change. Orders subject to approval.

REMEMBER!

- The free books and gift are mine to keep!
- There is no obligation!
- I may preview each shipment for 15 days!
- I can cancel anytime!

"Oh. You saw Uncle Cyrus with me outside."

The contrary thought popped into Gideon's head that it would have been nice if she'd prevaricated at least a little this time. He could have gotten mad and maybe vented some of his tension. Despite his earlier words to her, his vaunted patience was hanging by a thread; he wanted to understand her *now*, dammit, and it was driving him crazy to believe she was deliberately hiding something from him.

"I saw you with someone," he said finally.

"That was my uncle Cyrus. He's interesting looking, isn't he?"

Gideon didn't offer an opinion. "Since you haven't mentioned relatives living around here, I can't help but wonder what he was doing here."

"I asked him that. He and Aunt Julia—she's here, too, he said—moved to Oregon a while back, so I thought they'd be there. But they travel a lot."

"So what are they doing here?"

"He didn't say."

Gideon stared at her. "I thought you said you asked him?"

"Oh, I did. But he didn't answer. He's like that, I'm afraid. He's got the ears of a bat even though he's older than rocks, but he only answers the questions he wants to."

"Older than rocks?" Gideon ventured.

"Just an expression. But he is old. Very old, I think. I traced the family tree back as far as the turn of the century—and he wasn't on it yet."

"You're sure he's your uncle?"

"Well, no. That is, I'm sure we're related, I'm just not exactly clear how. Everybody else in the family is younger than he and Aunt Julia, I think, and we all call them aunt and uncle. However we're related, they *are* the heads of my family, we all agree with that."

Their drinks arrived, and Gideon took a healthy swallow of his. Fortified, he said carefully, "Is there any reason why you didn't introduce me to him?"

"You weren't out there."

"Maggie, why do I have the feeling you really would like it if I changed the subject?"

"Because you're perceptive?"

It was difficult for Gideon to get angry in the face of her hopeful air; in fact, he wanted to laugh. But various kinds of frustration could erode even the kindest of tempers—and his was hardly that. "I'm also stubborn," he told her. "It'll save time if you tell me what's going on."

"I don't think I want to do that. Have you noticed that we talk about time just the way we talk about money? We save time and spend it—save money and spend it."

"Are you making a point of some kind?"

"Not really, I guess. It was only a passing thought."

Gideon finished his drink. He wished that he'd ordered a double. "You obviously aren't willing to tell me what's going on. All right," he said. "Let's see if I can work it out on my own." He frowned at her for a moment, then shook his head. "Dammit, I can't. Give me a clue."

"I think the butler did it."

"Maggie."

She sipped her drink, watching him speculatively. "What makes you think something's going on?"

"Tension among the carnies that you could cut with a knife. A missing carny—and I checked Jasper's wagon, Maggie. All his things are there, and why did he leave them if he were going away for

good? The fact that you're clearly hiding something from me. And an itch at the back of my
neck that tells me I'm being watched every moment I'm at the encampment."

Her eyes widened slightly, then turned thoughtful. "Being watched? You should be used to that
by now, I'd think; they all watch you."

"I don't mean it that way. I mean there's someone watching me on the sly—someone who's taking a hell of a lot of trouble to make sure he
doesn't get caught at it."

"Even today after we made the announcement?"

"Yes."

Maggie didn't like that. She didn't like that at
all. Her innocent expression began to change. If
Gideon was right—and he didn't strike her as
paranoid—then her quarry considered him a threat
apart from his ownership of the carnival. But
why? She couldn't come up with a single answer
to that question. But there was one answer she
was sure of. If Gideon was a threat, he'd have to
know about it so that he would be on guard.

"Maggie?" The chameleon had changed colors
again, he realized. Her eyes were direct and clear,
her features almost imperceptibly sharper. This
face matched the mind he had suspected lurked
underneath all the layers: quick, intelligent, serious, and quite rational.

She braced herself mentally and kept her voice
quiet when she began to talk. "I wasn't going to
tell you because I think I know how you'll react.
But it looks as though you need to be aware of
some things."

"What things?"

"A few weeks ago a member of the carnival,
missing for a while, was found dead . . . at the

bottom of an old, abandoned well. The police decided his death was accidental, that he'd fallen in, maybe in the dark. They were satisfied with their conclusion."

"But you weren't?" Gideon was watching her intently.

"I wasn't with the carnival then. But the man who was killed was a cousin of mine. Merlin."

"Sean's Merlin?"

Something shifted in the back of Maggie's mind, gone too quickly for her to grasp it. But it would come clear sooner or later, she thought. She hoped. "Yes," she said. "My aunt Julia decided he'd been murdered."

"She's his mother?"

"No. Or at least, I don't think so. She's never said she was."

Gideon blinked. "Another vague connection?"

"I suppose."

He drew a deep breath. "But she decided he'd been murdered. She was with the carnival?"

"No, she was in Oregon." The expression on her face and in her voice was still serious, in comparison to which the words were lunatic. Gideon sent a glance down at his empty glass, wishing again that he'd ordered a double. He took a moment to try to find a logical thread. He failed. "Why did she decide he'd been murdered? I mean, what led her to believe that his death wasn't accidental?"

A faint glint of sympathy shone in Maggie's eyes. "It sounds absurd, I know. All I can tell you is that my aunt Julia's pronouncements are rarely—and I do mean rarely—wrong. If my aunt Julia told me the sun rose in the west, I'd believe her until I found evidence to the contrary."

"All right, I'll accept that since I don't seem to have a choice. She decided he'd been murdered. And then?"

"She called me."

"Why?"

"Because I'm the logical member of the family," Maggie said.

He stared at her.

"Well, I am. And I'm very good at solving puzzles and problems. I've become sort of a troubleshooter for the family over the past few years. So, naturally, she called me."

Deciding to ignore her claims of logic for the moment, Gideon said carefully, "Do you mean your aunt sent you to look for a killer?"

Maggie nodded gravely. "Well, Cousin Merlin's spirit could never be at peace until his murder was solved. Aunt Julia didn't want him chained to that awful well for eternity. Think how bored he'd be."

"Maggie, you don't really believe that stuff?" His question was cautious.

"It doesn't matter what I believe. Cousin Merlin believed it. And Aunt Julia says it's always safer to hedge your bets, so she's willing to accept the possibility. So, on the possibility that he was right, we owe it to Cousin Merlin to resolve his death and set him free."

It was said with such reasonable understanding that Gideon was more or less forced to accept it.

"All right," he said slowly. "For whatever reason, your aunt sent you to the carnival to find a murderer."

"Yes."

"And have you?"

"Not exactly. But I'm working on it."

"*How* are you working on it?"

"There wasn't much I could do at first except watch and listen. Merlin was well liked and didn't have a temper to speak of, so I doubt he made somebody mad enough to kill him. He was an old man. A very kind and honest man. So why would anybody want to murder him? I couldn't think what the motive might be until something you said today rang a bell."

"What did I say?"

"You called the carnival a sanctuary. I started to think about it, and I realized that it would be a good place for somebody to hide if they'd committed a crime."

"What kind of crime?"

"My bet is a profitable one, with the spoils valuable enough to make murder worthwhile. Otherwise, why bother? I think Merlin found out something and threatened the killer with exposure. He would have done that; he was always honest."

She frowned briefly. "Suppose you'd stolen something valuable and decided to lie low until the statute of limitations ran out. A carnival would be a good place to hide. Very good, in fact. Always on the move, in costume whenever you wanted to be, and plenty of places to hide the goods."

"But carnies are suspicious of outsiders," Gideon objected.

"Right. Which means that either you'd have to be familiar with the life, or else be good enough to fake it."

"Like you," Gideon murmured.

She smiled. "Like me. You would also have been a part of Wonderland no longer than seven years; if you've hidden a fortune in one of the wagons or cages, you wouldn't want to wait any longer than necessary to claim it."

"That's logical as far as it goes," he admitted. "But you don't know what was stolen, where it was stolen, how long ago it was stolen. Your assumption is based on the theory there was that initial theft."

"I know, it's a shaky long shot. But it's all I've got. I checked the Wonderland books and found two people who've been with the carnival less than seven years."

"Who are they?"

She hesitated. "I'd rather not tell you yet. Wait a minute," she added when he opened his mouth to speak. "I've got a very good reason."

"Which is?"

"With the best intentions of being objective, I've still come to know those people. And that knowledge might be coloring my ideas of who the killer could be. You don't know them; you'll be more objective. Until we have something that points specifically to one person, I'd rather you consider the whole problem with a completely open mind. If you're suspicious of everyone, you might notice something I've missed."

" 'Problem'? Murder?"

"It's as good a word as any. Do you agree?"

"Not with the word—but I suppose you're right not to give me the names. For now, anyway."

"Good."

He nodded. "So, you found the names. And then?"

"I noted down where the carnival was when they joined up, along with the exact dates they arrived. Uncle Cyrus is checking that out for me."

"Looking for thefts?"

"I need a few facts. All I've got so far is wildly speculative and based, as you said, on the assumption that behind at least one murder is a thief protecting his cache."

"At least one murder? You think he's killed again?" Gideon frowned, then said, "Jasper."

"I hope he's wandered off. I really do hope so. But if he found out something he shouldn't have. . . ."

"Go to the police," Gideon said flatly.

"And tell them what?" She steadily held his gaze. "We have a carny who's been missing, for certain, only since this morning, not even twenty-four hours. We have a death weeks ago that the police in another state judged to be accidental. And that's all we have."

"I don't like it, Maggie."

"Neither do I. Especially if somebody's watching you."

He thought about that for a moment. "Why me?"

"Exactly. I thought at first that you'd be a threat to the killer if you planned to break up the carnival. That made sense; he wouldn't want to lose his handy hiding place. It's also one of the reasons I was so hard on you. If you'd announced you were going to sell out piecemeal, he might have panicked; there goes his nifty hiding place, and *you* were responsible for the loss. But that wasn't the announcement you made today. And if he still considers you a threat, the question is definitely why. I don't know the answer. Do you?"

"Natural anxiety? I'm a stranger and therefore a threat? Or maybe it's a more personal threat."

"What do you mean?"

"Did you dent any hearts before I came along?"

The question was light, but the expression in his eyes was sombér.

"Not that I know of," she answered immediately. "And I think you're on the wrong track."

"Maybe. But if I'm a threat to the killer because of what he's done—then how? All the people in the carnival were total strangers to me when I arrived. Even my connection to Balthazar was so vague I'm still not sure we were related at all. What could I know about all this?"

Maggie shook her head slightly. "I don't know." She hesitated, then added, "But it might be a good idea if we had a very public fight and you went away for a few days."

"No," he said instantly. "I'm not leaving unless you go with me."

"Is that a proposition?" she asked in a mild tone.

"For want of a better term—yes. Come with me. I have a terrific penthouse overlooking the Bay. Maid service, cable TV, and a Jaguar that doesn't live in a cage."

"You sweet talker you," she murmured, thinking that if he were ever earnest about that offer, she'd find it impossible to turn him down.

He had to laugh, but shook his head. "I'm serious, Maggie. You have no business trying to catch a murderer."

She thought about how to explain this to him and kept her voice quiet and firm. "I have family business, Gideon. Family is very important to me. A member of my family was killed because of greed or panic, and I can't just let that go. I have a responsibility to find out what happened."

"It isn't your responsibility—"

"Yes, it is. I made it mine."

"And what if the killer's on to you?" He reached across the table and covered one of her hands with his. "You're the real threat to him. The only threat, as far as I can see. And if this maniac could push a kind old man into a well, I doubt he'd balk at killing a beautiful young woman."

"You think he should get off free?"

Gideon swore softly. "No. We can hire a private investigator to look into it."

"Who wouldn't be able to get near the carnies. Gideon, they're already nervous and suspicious. When Merlin's body was found, the police were all over the carnival. I told you some of their stories; *most* of them are hiding. From their pasts, if nothing else. One of the reasons none of them wanted you to know about Jasper is because they were afraid you'd call in the police; that's why everyone kept saying he was in town. If another stranger showed up now, they'd close ranks so tightly we'd never find out the truth. And what about the killer? How would he react?"

"You're in danger, don't you understand that?" The general frustration Gideon was feeling had found an outlet, and it was all the stronger because he felt a chill of fear for her.

"He isn't on to me, Gideon; I'm sure he's not. I'm carny, remember? I fit right in. Nobody knows the connection between me and Merlin. I haven't asked anyone the wrong questions or ransacked the wagons, or otherwise done anything to make myself look suspicious."

She had backed into a corner. And he didn't like it one little bit. "You seem to know everyone's history. Didn't you find out by asking them about themselves?"

"No. They felt comfortable enough to tell me. Carnies don't ask questions of each other."

"Maggie—"

"Look, there's nothing else to be done until Uncle Cyrus dredges up a few facts, something he's very good at. In the meantime, why don't we try to forget about it? We're miles from the carnival, and even if the killer rode one of the horses, he couldn't possibly be near right now."

"I'm going to do my best to change your mind about leaving the carnival," he warned.

"Fine," she said easily despite a number of misgivings; she thought that if he tried hard enough, she'd have a difficult time resisting him. "But I don't want to talk about it anymore right now. You promised me a dance."

Gideon had just pushed his chair back and was about to rise when a sudden commotion near the foyer drew their attention. The door banged, startled sounds rent the air as well as several creative curses, and a mottled-brown blur shot into the lounge, bounded over the piano, and skidded to a stop beside Gideon. The creature wore a red collar with rhinestones and a silver tag that said he belonged to the Wonderland carnival.

"Oh, hell," Gideon muttered.

Leo reared up, paws on his idol's thigh, and chattered insistently in his peculiar language.

'Gideon ignored him. He looked at Maggie. "What'd he do, run all the way?"

"He probably stowed away in the car. I forgot to check the back before we left, and the windows were down."

"What's he saying to me?"

"That it's hot out in the car. And he's thirsty."

Lifting an eyebrow at her, Gideon said, "That's

just common sense; you don't really understand him."

Maggie sipped her tomato juice placidly.

"Look, cat," he began, shifting his gaze to the animal, then broke off as their waitress approached stiffly.

"Sir, unless that is a Seeing Eye dog, it isn't allowed in here," she announced.

Gideon silently debated, but didn't think he could get away with the fiction. Leo wasn't wearing a harness.

Leo swiveled his head around to stare at her, and she stepped back, disconcerted. The bored young man at the piano hadn't missed a beat even when the cat had soared over his baby grand. The other patrons were ruthlessly minding their own business.

"It's hot outside," Gideon said, going with the flow. "And he's thirsty."

"The manager says—"

"I'll speak to the manager." Gideon pushed the cat's paws off his thigh and rose. "You will excuse me?" he said to Maggie in a wry tone.

"Certainly."

"Thank you. Leo, get in the chair." To his surprise, the cat instantly hopped into his vacated chair and sat down. Gideon stared at him for an instant, then added sternly, "And keep your nose out of my glass."

Leo assumed a saintly expression.

Judging the worth of that, Gideon made a rude noise under his breath and followed the retreating waitress.

Maggie was left laughing softly to herself and thinking that any man who could hold his own with a scene-stealer like Leo was an unusual man indeed.

The manager had arguments ranging from the feelings of other patrons to the requirements of the health inspector, but a small bribe and the promise that Leo would not enter the restaurant won his grudging acceptance. He even offered a bowl of milk—though it cost as much as a double scotch.

Gideon carried the bowl back to the table since the waitress had taken one look and sneered. He couldn't decide whether to leave her an extra large tip to show he was above such trite emotions as revenge, or leave no tip at all to teach her a needed lesson in manners. He was still silently debating the question when he reached the table. He snagged an extra chair from a nearby table and placed it at their own, correctly deciding that Leo's feelings would be hurt if he couldn't sit up at the table with his expensive drink like people.

"Here, you misbegotten animal," he said, removing his glass from in front of Leo and replacing it with the bowl. Then he placed the new chair closer to Maggie's and sat down himself as the cat began to drink thirstily.

"He's in grace?" she asked.

"Until we go into the restaurant. Then he's going back to the car. Or maybe the trunk. He didn't stick his nose in my glass, did he?"

"He was a perfect gentleman."

Gideon sighed. "I have a feeling we differ on our definitions of that, but never mind."

"It was nice of you to bribe the manager. Leo appreciates it. And so do I."

"My good deed for the day. Do you think he'll insist on dancing with us?"

"He's tone-deaf."

After looking at her for a minute, Gideon rubbed a vague ache between his eyes with his thumb, murmuring, "You know, for a while there—a brief while—you hardly said anything absurd at all. Well, I mean, it was all absurd, but it made a crazy kind of sense. Except for that stuff about a murderer's hiding out in the carnival and slinking around guarding his secreted treasure. That was absurd, but you made it sound so reasonable that I actually thought it made sense."

Maggie reached over to pat his hand where it rested on the table. "I think you're losing it."

Still staring at her, he caught her hand between both his and said in the same lucid tone, "You remember what I said about a hundred years ago? The part about my being a patient man, and being willing to wait until I got all my questions answered?"

"It sounds familiar, yes."

"That was a reasonable thing for me to say, wasn't it?"

She nodded.

He nodded as well. "And that's what's wrong with it. Maggie, my date was just crashed by a cat. Is that reasonable?"

She cleared her throat. "I suppose not."

"I'm sleeping in a tent in the middle of Kansas. A tent I had to buy because I had to bend my knees in the first one. A tent pitched in the middle of a carnival, which, to put it mildly, is a little strange even for carnivals. Is that reasonable?"

Maggie used her free hand to prop up her chin. "Well, when you put it like that . . ."

"I'm involved with a woman who has the eyes of a siren, the face of an angel, and a mind like a labyrinth. She offers absurd answers to the most logical questions, and changes mood right in front of my eyes, and I *know* she's a bit mad; I just don't know to what degree. She's trying to find one maniac in the middle of a rolling asylum, because the maniac pushed her cousin into a well."

"Gideon—"

"Yes, I know you think it's reasonable. But it isn't. Nothing in this entire situation is reasonable, not even our conversations, and certainly not our relationship. I'm a rational man; I know reason when I see it. There isn't any. So why am I trying to be reasonable?"

Maggie cleared her throat. "The need to impose order on chaos?" she offered.

He looked briefly distracted, even interested in a mild way, but then shook his head. "Control is an illusion, I know that. Order is an illusion. With the possible exception of mathematical formulas, there's no such thing as pure logic."

"And so?" she murmured.

"Back to my original question. Why am I trying to be reasonable and logical?"

"Because you're a rational man?" Maggie had the somewhat unnerving feeling that whatever sense of control she'd believed she possessed in this situation with Gideon had definitely been an illusion.

"But that's where I went wrong. I can't live in your world and play by the rules in mine."

"Meaning?"

"Let's dance," he said.

Pulled gently from her chair and led out onto a

deserted dance floor, Maggie said, "You didn't answer my question."

Gideon drew her into his arms, sending an automatically wary glance back toward their table to make sure Leo was sitting blamelessly in his chair. Looking down at Maggie, he said, "I've decided to play by your rules, that's all."

"My rules? I didn't know I had any."

"That," he said, "is what's so nice about it. I had no idea rules were so confining. Why didn't you tell me?"

"I needed an edge," she said involuntarily.

He eyes gleamed. "Well, we're on equal ground now. No rules. We'll just play it by ear."

Maggie wanted to think of a way to argue him out of his position, mostly because as long as he'd stood by his gentlemanly patience she had indeed had an edge. But now, if he truly intended to let rationality and patience go by the board, she didn't stand a chance. All her talk of chemical reactions and getting questions answered wasn't going to hold him at arm's length now.

Rules said that you took your time and did things in their proper order; without rules, all that was left to follow were your instincts.

And how on earth could she fight when her instincts demanded she respond to *his* instincts?

She couldn't. From the moment he had said *I want you* with such deep conviction in his tone of voice, she had known that fate had stepped into her life. She had waited for the right man, knowing he would come. And he had. All her uncertainties and wariness couldn't hide that from her.

To give herself to a man was to give all that she was, she knew. It wasn't true of all women, but it was of her. She thought that Gideon could love her if he'd let himself, but if it never happened, it still wouldn't change her feelings.

When that certain knowledge rose in her, Maggie characteristically turned away from uncertainty. It was done; there was no going back now. And she knew love was something one treated with respect, something fierce and powerful that left its mark wherever it passed.

"You've gone very quiet," he murmured, pulling her a little closer as the beat of the music slowed.

Maggie slid her arms up around his neck and sighed as his hands settled at her hips. He would be rather fun without the rule book, she thought. There was a cockeyed sense of humor inside him, probably set aside at an early age but still there. If Gideon gave himself half a chance, she believed he would make a pretty fair chameleon himself. She hoped they'd get a chance to explore the possibility.

In the meantime, however, this impulsive conclusion of his was dangerous. Not the conclusion itself—but the timing. And she had to warn him of consequences, because she didn't believe he was ready to accept them. He had to know; it was only fair. Perhaps he wanted only passion for the time being, but he had to know it would change them both.

Conversationally, she said, "I was just thinking that this whole situation is worse than you know."

"In what way?" he asked warily.

"I'm afraid I love you."

Gideon stopped moving and stared down at her. He looked a little bemused, but something was kindling in his eyes. "You're afraid you love me? We met yesterday."

"That hardly matters."

"You're *afraid* you love me," he repeated slowly.

"Well, yes. If it were mere passion, there wouldn't really be a problem, because that's a fleeting thing. When it was over, you'd go back to San Francisco and I'd go to Richmond, and that would be it. But love is different. So I thought I'd better warn you."

"Warn me?"

Maggie's smile was a little rueful. "Gideon, my family's unusual in a number of ways. Strange ways, I suppose. There are certain patterns in our lives, almost as if somebody planned it all out. And one of the patterns is that there has never been an unhappy love affair or a divorce since before the turn of the century. It seems to be stamped in our cells to fall in love only once . . . and with the right person."

Gideon had forgotten about the music. Holding her in his arms, staring down at her, he asked carefully, "What are you saying, Maggie?"

Her expression was entirely serious now, her eyes direct and sober. Her soft, childlike voice was certain. "What I'm saying is that once we become lovers, you're mine. You'll belong to me in the same way that I'll belong to you. Not a summer fling, not an affair, nothing temporary. That's one of the answers you were looking for, Gideon. In my world, love is forever."

After a moment he began moving again to the music. She danced very well, he noted idly. And she *fit* him very well; there was nothing awkward in how they moved together, nothing uncertain or clumsy. He wondered if their lovemaking would be so gracefully complete.

"I would say you can't be serious," he said finally. "But I think you are."

"Oh, yes, I'm serious."

"And if I said that all *I* want is an affair?"

"It wouldn't matter." Her voice was serene now, her fey eyes smiling gently up at him. "You could leave me, of course, once it was over. Walk away and never look back. And I wouldn't chase after you. But you'd still be mine. Other women would know it. And so would you."

"Witchcraft?" he said dryly, about half serious.

"Love. Real love changes you, brands you inside and out. Whether you feel it or someone else feels it for you doesn't matter; you're still branded."

"Maggie, is this some kind of new strategy? I mean, do you expect me to run screaming into the night?"

"I don't expect anything from you except honesty, because that's exactly what I'm offering you. I didn't plan it, and the timing could have been better, but there doesn't seem to be much I can do about that now. I love you, Gideon."

"It was much pleasanter at home,"
thought poor Alice,
"when one wasn't always growing
larger and smaller,

I almost wish I hadn't gone down
that rabbit-hole—
and yet—and yet—it's rather curious, you know,
this sort of life!"

Six

Gideon didn't know what to say. He gazed down into her face, and it was the face that had in so short a time become so fascinating to him, the face that haunted even his dreams. The face that was, now, serene and nakedly vulnerable, unmasked, unguarded.

Innocent.

My God, he thought, *she can't be*—"You've never been in love before?" he asked slowly.

"No."

"Then . . . that is . . . you've never—?"

"No," she answered steadily.

As he'd told her earlier, he hadn't really thought much beyond today. To become her lover—yes, he wanted that. He wanted that so badly that his first impulse was to ignore her warning. But in his life, professional and personal, every risk tended to be weighed carefully before an action was taken. And even though he had decided to play by her lack of rules, he couldn't ignore his basic intellectual way of viewing and dealing with the world.

To be her first lover . . . He'd heard it said that a woman never forgot her first lover; was that what she meant? They would both be marked by the taking of innocence? No, he thought. Nothing so simple.

"You're saying I'll hurt you," he said. The music stopped then. Appropriate, Gideon thought.

"No, that isn't what I'm saying." Maggie stepped back and away from him, then turned and preceded him from the dance floor. When they were sitting at their table again, she reached over to pat Leo's drowsy head. "He's half asleep. The milk, I guess."

"Maggie, look at me."

She did, smiling. "I'm not saying you'll hurt me, Gideon. At least not intentionally. I'm just saying that, for me, you're forever. And despite my flaky appearance, I'm quite conventional about some things. Romantic, I suppose. I've waited this long because no man was forever. You are. There won't be anyone else for me."

"You can't know that."

"Of course I can. I told you. We only love once. Like wolves and hawks, we mate for life. If you consider that a burden, then you'd better go back to San Francisco now."

"You're just trying to get me away from the carnival for a while," he said, hoping that was it.

Her smile faded, and she shook her head slightly. "No. And I don't want you to think it. Gideon, finding Merlin's killer is important to me, but you're more important. I don't want you to leave, even though I don't like the fact that somebody's watching you, and I'd probably have an easier job of it if you did go. But I'm talking about the two of us, not what's going on around us. And I'm not playing a game, with or without rules. I'm simply telling you the truth."

"That you love me."

She nodded. "That I love you."

He eyed her. "Will I sleep in your wagon tonight?"

"If you want to."

"In your bed?"

"I'd like that," she said simply, with all the trusting anticipation of innocent longing.

Gideon yanked his gaze away from her and stared at his empty glass. He thought of ordering another drink, but discarded the impulse. Dutch courage wasn't going to help, he decided. "You are the most contrary woman I've ever met," he muttered. "Yesterday, you said we were moving too fast. Or I was."

"That was yesterday."

"I see. Today, you love me, and you say it's forever."

"It is."

He sighed and glanced at his watch. Odd. Minutes ago, he thought he had figured out how to respond to Maggie and her world—throw out the rule book and act on impulse. But all his impulses seemed to be scrambled. Baffled and more than a little unnerved, he was back where he'd started and with an additional feeling of responsibility because it meant so much to her. How much did it mean to him?

She was offering what he'd said he wanted—for them to be lovers. Yet, at the same time, she was saying that it was serious for her, that it had to be, because she loved him. She was making a commitment.

Gideon felt more than a little wary of her prediction that her love would change him, mark him forever. If any other woman had said it, he doubted he'd believe it at all; he'd consider it only words, nice romantic words that sounded lovely and faded in the face of reality. But Maggie had said those words, said them with utter certainty. With no tinge of possessiveness in her voice she'd said that he would belong to her, and she to him. She meant it, believed it.

He had a feeling he should too.

So he couldn't just reach for what he wanted without counting the cost to Maggie . . . and perhaps to himself. He owed it to them both to be completely aware of the consequences. If he couldn't believe at least that they had a future together, then he had no right to be in her bed.

"Gideon?"

"Our table should be ready," he said abruptly. "I'll take Leo back out to the car, and then we can eat."

"Fine," she said agreeably.

Tina was sitting on the steps of her wagon when Gideon's rented car returned to the encampment. It was nearly nine, but summer's dusk provided enough light to see clearly. She watched them get out, saw Leo bound from the backseat.

He *had* been with them. Lamont owed her a dollar; she'd guessed right. The cat hurried toward her, and she silently moved aside to let him into her wagon where his food dish was.

Maggie spoke briefly to Gideon, who nodded, and then she went off toward the animals to do her nightly check. Tina kept her gaze on Gideon, watching as he strolled toward Maggie's wagon and then stood looking at his new tent. He wasn't a man who gave away much, Tina thought, but it was obvious he was struggling with a knotty problem. After a thoughtful moment Tina rose and made her way over to Maggie's wagon.

The rest of the camp was fairly quiet with everyone settling down for the night; the only sounds were of Sean, Buster, and Richie—the carnival's only other youngster, whose parents ran the refreshments concession—tossing a football near the edge of the woods.

Reaching Maggie's wagon, Tina leaned against one of the rear wheels and studied Gideon's brooding face. "Hi," she offered. "Have a nice dinner?"

He looked up from his baleful contemplation of the new tent and half nodded. "Sure."

"I hope Leo didn't cause problems."

"None to speak of."

"He wasn't the one, huh?"

After a moment Gideon said, "Does it show so plainly?"

"Only around the edges." Apparently going off on a tangent, Tina said, "You know, I gave Maggie a reading when she first joined the carnival."

"Reading?"

"Madame Valentina knows all," she said with only a slight hint of mockery. "Crystal balls, tea leaves, tarot cards."

"A scam," Gideon said dryly.

She was unoffended. "Maybe. Sometimes. But I always like to leave room for possibilities. Gypsy blood will tell, I guess. Because sometimes I see past the props. With Maggie, I definitely did."

"All right, I'll bite," he said. "What did you see?"

"A mirror."

He frowned a little. "I don't get it."

"I didn't either, at first," Tina admitted. "But

then I watched Maggie for a few days. And I realized that she was always what people expected her to be, an instant reflection of their idea of what she was. Just like a mirror."

Gideon didn't believe in fortune-telling, but the observation made sense, and Tina's conclusions sounded so right that he felt a sudden, odd shift inside himself as if things were rapidly falling into place. "I thought of her as a chameleon," he said slowly.

"That's true, as far as it goes. She changes to suit her surroundings. I imagine she'd fit into place almost anywhere you'd care to name."

"A born actress?"

"No, it's more than that. Much more complicated in fact. Hers isn't simply an outward change; she *becomes* different inside—or opens up a new part of herself. It's completely instinctive and probably unconscious, although I'm sure she knows the ability is hers." Tina smiled slightly. "You would have understood it in time, I think."

"Then why tell me?"

Softly, she said, "Because I saw your face in the mirror."

"What?"

She nodded. "Weeks ago. I knew you'd be the one—maybe the only one—to reach past the reflection. Gideon, we all need to be seen as we truly are by at least one other person. Until you can look at Maggie without your ideas of what she is getting in the way, you'll never see her clearly. Until you look at her with no expectations, she'll always reflect your ideas of her."

"That doesn't make sense," Gideon said. "I *want* to see her clearly. Dammit, that's what I've been trying to do almost every moment since I got here!"

"And she's trying to help you. Fighting her own nature. That's why she baffles you. The problem with you two is that it's all happening too fast, with no time to think, and you believe that's what you need to do."

"Think? Of course I should think about this."

Tina shook her head slightly. "Thinking about love isn't going to help you. It's an emotion, re- member? An instinct. The mind looks for reasons and explanations. The heart just feels. Maggie is a creature of instinct and emotion, Gideon; what she *feels* will always be more important than what she thinks. What you *think* of her is getting in the way. Why don't you try feeling about her? You might be surprised."

He stared at her for a long moment, then said abruptly, "What's your story, Tina? Why are you here?"

"Have you heard the saying that shrinks are always crazier than their patients?" She waited for his nod, then said cheerfully, "I have a doctor- ate in psychiatry. I worked in a mental hospital. One day about eight years ago I decided I'd better leave. Good night, Gideon." She turned and strolled off in the direction of her wagon.

He gazed after her, wondering why he wasn't surprised.

Was Tina right about him and Maggie? His mind was telling him the whole thing was absurd, lunatic, yet it felt right. Felt . . . Was that the problem? Was his rational mind so insistent on reasoning everything out that his instincts and emotions were clouded? In trying so hard to understand Maggie, had he closed down the only part of him that *could* understand her?

Throw out the rule book and act on impulse. . . .

He hadn't been able to do it. To announce it, yes, to say to himself that was the way to cope. Then Maggie had said she loved him. Why? Why then? Because, he realized slowly, she knew where impulse would lead him. She knew they'd be lovers. Her own feelings made a simple physical relationship impossible, so she had to warn him, stop him before he followed impulse into an emotional tangle that would hurt them both.

Throw out the rule book—yes. But impulse? No. So far, his impulses had come from physical desire and mental frustration; he hadn't let himself feel except with his senses.

Maggie's a creature of instinct and emotion. . . . And he was a rational man, a man whose work dealt with numbers and logic and carefully calculated risks. A man whose life had followed the safe, well-traveled pathways.

Until now. With no road to guide him, no compass that didn't whirl madly, he had tried to cling to logic and reason, and found both failing him at every turn.

"Gideon?"

Maggie had appeared from around the end of the wagon. Looking fiercely at her, he said somewhat violently, "God, you're complicated!"

She blinked, then smiled. "I'm sorry. I would say I never promised you a rose garden, but I've never understood why that's supposed to be easy. Gardens are hard work, especially when they're filled with roses. Because they're pretty, I suppose, and pleasant. Still, they have lots of thorns."

"I'm in the middle of a crisis," Gideon said, "and you're talking about roses."

"It was just a thought," she explained apologetically. "I didn't intend to belittle your crisis. You have had a rough day, haven't you?"

"I've had better, let's say. Has Jasper come back?"

"No, there's been no sign of him. The others expect he'll be back by morning. Maybe he will."

"You don't believe that."

"Maybe he will," she repeated steadily.

After a moment Gideon crossed the space to the steps of her wagon and sat down. It was getting dark now, but there was a full moon and he could see her easily. "Did you know Tina had a doctorate?" he asked conversationally.

"Yes."

"In psychiatry?"

"Yes. Have you been on her couch?"

"Something like that." He sighed. "So were you . . . in absentia."

"Oh. Any insights?"

"Plenty. That's why I said you're complicated. Maggie, why do you love me?"

She looked at him gravely. "I haven't asked myself the question, Gideon. Why should I? If something exists, it is. The reasons aren't important."

"I wish I understood that." He got to his feet slowly. "Until I do, I guess I'd better sleep in the tent. Good night, Maggie."

"Good night."

The watcher kept close to the shadows of a wagon on the other side of the camp, still and silent as the two he observed parted outside her wagon. It had been too light for him to get any nearer to them without risking being discovered, so he hadn't been able to hear what they were saying.

Was he still safe? Gideon Hughes was the danger, but *she* baffled him; her sudden arrival at the carnival had made him definitely nervous. He'd thought her a flake at first, but weeks of her presence had told him different. Not dumb, no, not dumb at all. Not crazy, either, not like most of the others here. He had worried about her . . . until Hughes came.

Fate was against him, that was it. What other possible reason could there be for Hughes to show up so damned far from San Francisco? It wasn't fair. Who could have guessed that a man like him would be in any way connected with something as bizarre as Wonderland? He'd remember. Sooner or later he'd remember, make the connection.

Heart thudding, the watcher made himself calm down. It was all right. Doubtful that Hughes knew about Merlin, and as for Jasper, he was just missing, that was all. Damn the old man for coming up missing just when the last thing he wanted was more questions asked! And there was something odd he had noticed that he didn't like. Carnies talked among themselves, sharing a liking for speculation and gossip—but nobody was talking about Merlin. At least not to him. He had the uneasy feeling that was a bad sign; they might not be able to be certain the old man's death wasn't an accident, but they were all suspicious enough to be silent on the matter—and tense about it.

He had to stay calm, not panic. Everything would be all right if he didn't panic and do something stupid. He glanced around warily, then slipped from the shadows and moved silently back toward his own place.

A few moments later, another—much smaller—shadow darted between the wagons until it reached one with the door open and light spilling out.

"Sean," Tina said sternly as the boy came in, "I've told you not to wander around out there in the dark."

"It ain't dark, Ma. Moon's up. You can see out there like it was daylight. Almost, anyway."

"Well, never mind. Wash up and get ready for bed."

All the privacy of a goldfish, Maggie thought vaguely as she got ready for bed. It was hardly surprising that Tina had offered her insights to Gideon, especially considering the life she used to live. The only surprise was that the others hadn't gotten in on the courtship. On second thought, Maggie wasn't surprised by that, either; the tension in the carnival was distracting everybody.

That tension wasn't helping Gideon. Even worse, Maggie knew it would probably be several days—if then—before Uncle Cyrus found any information of use to them. They could do nothing except wait.

Maggie crawled into bed and blew out her lamp, wondering with a heart-clenching pang if Gideon would stay now or if she had lost him by telling the truth. He was off balance and troubled by it, and he was not the kind of man who could accept that state of mind for long. He'd accused her of being complicated—and it *had* been an accusation —but he was no less complex. An honorable man, or he'd be in her bed right now. Humorous enough to play straight man to a cat. A man who wanted things to make sense . . . even when they didn't.

The problem was that love didn't make sense. Maggie knew. It wasn't a reasoned thing, a calculated thing. She had no idea why it was Gideon she loved rather than any of the men she had known over the years. She hadn't a clue as to which quality or qualities of his had touched something deep inside her.

All she knew was that she loved him.

Ever since she'd admitted to him that she was in love with him, she had held a tight rein on her own emotions. As a child, Maggie had more than once suffered because she felt things so deeply, because feelings *mattered* so much to her. What she remembered most clearly from her earliest childhood weren't scenes or objects, or even people —just emotions so intense they'd been shattering. She had quite literally made herself sick with excitement or joy, grief or pain.

The years had brought a certain amount of control, naturally, but even now when her feelings became so intense they were painful, she had learned to turn away, to deflect them until she had time to breathe, to calm down. At such moments her mind darted off on tangents, schooled to shy away from intensity.

She wondered if Gideon had thought she was being flippant with her vague talk of rose gardens. But she'd wanted so badly to throw her arms around him, to let the wild feelings inside her burst out where there was room for them. As a child, the strength of her emotions had caused adults to step back in surprise, shaken by the intensity her small body held; but what was inside her now made everything else she had ever felt pale by comparison.

You're saying I'll hurt you.

She hadn't wanted him to believe that, unwilling to use a very real kind of emotional blackmail. He would hurt her if he left, she knew, hurt her in a way a part of her wouldn't survive, but it wasn't his fault. If he couldn't love her, then he couldn't; he wasn't to blame. To tie a man's heart with pity and guilt was not only cruel, it was tragic, and she wanted no part of it no matter what the cost to her.

Maggie turned onto her back and stared at the dark ceiling, unconsciously pressing both hands to her middle underneath the covers as if she could hold it in. It. The violence of feeling that was like madness.

She hardly slept that night, but rose at dawn to feed the animals. Farley joined her when she was half finished, kilted and cheerful as always, scolding her for dragging a heavy bag of feed out of the supply wagon.

"I'm not as puny as I look," she said mildly, watching as he tossed the bag easily over his shoulder.

He paused to eye her thoughtfully. " 'Puny' isn't the word I'd use, lass. But you do seem a mite pale this mornin', and that's a fact. Bad night?"

"A bout of insomnia." She shrugged. "It happens. We should exercise the animals today, they're getting fat."

"Another fact. Start after breakfast?"

Maggie nodded. "I'll do the cats if you'll handle the rest."

"Right. The horses have grazed down a nice clearing for the big cage; I'll set it up for you."

"Thanks, Farley." She watched him carry the bag of feed toward the monkeys' cage, then got a small bag of seed and went to feed the birds. She had just finished and was vacantly watching them settle down to eat when Gideon's quiet voice came from behind her.

"Good morning."

She turned to look at him, a bit surprised to realize he'd been up for some time. He had obviously showered and shaved; his hair was still damp. He was wearing jeans and a dark blue T-shirt, the casual clothes making him look rougher, maybe even a little dangerous. And there was something in his eyes, a dark, inward-turned look she'd never seen before.

"Good morning." She was glad her voice was calm; she certainly didn't feel that way. She wanted to hide away somewhere, to catch her breath and find a way to cope with the emotions. And she didn't want him to touch her. If he touched her, she'd never be able to do it, she was barely in control *now*.

Gideon's faithful shadow was at his heels, and she latched onto the distraction gratefully. "Good morning, Leo."

"Wooo," Leo returned politely.

"He slept outside my tent," Gideon said, his voice holding a lightness that seemed a bit forced. "And he dreamed. I didn't know cats dreamed. He must have been chasing rabbits."

Leo chattered briefly but emphatically, tilting his head to stare up at his idol.

"Rats, then," Gideon said, abstracted now.

Maggie blinked. Odd. She had mentally decided that Leo had said just that. Not that one could be sure of a cat's meaning, but it had *felt* right to her. Gideon didn't seem to be aware that he had translated Leo's forceful correction about the rats.

"Are you all right?" he asked abruptly.

The question startled her. "I'm fine. Ready for breakfast, though," she added. "Tina should have it prepared by now. Let me put this seed back in the wagon." She went immediately to do that, wondering if she was going to be able to get through this without doing something stupid.

Gideon joined her silently, and by tacit consent they ate their breakfasts out in the open near Tina's wagon rather than in Maggie's.

That set the tone for the entire day. Maggie kept herself busy, distracting her mind as much as possible; Gideon remained near for the most part, watching her. Always watching her. She felt his steady gaze and was surprised to realize she had absolutely no idea what he was thinking or feeling—or even what he expected of her. It might have been the strength of her own emotions blinding her, she decided; whatever the reason, her knack of sensing had apparently deserted her.

It was unnerving.

Gideon talked to most of the carnies that day, but hardly at all to Maggie. Whenever he got near her, she always seemed to be just starting some new task designed to occupy her attention fully. It began with the cats—the lions, tiger, and cheetah— all of which were exercised one at a time in a big cage some little distance from the encampment.

The cats were walked on leashes from their own cages to the exercise enclosure, allowed a few minutes to prowl and get the kinks out of their legs, and then Maggie went in with each to put it through a few simple tricks.

Gideon didn't like it. He thought Farley should have been doing this, but the kilted redhead was exercising the horses; apparently, some division of labor had been decided upon. Granted, Maggie was good with the cats, Gideon could see that.

And they obeyed her with no snarls or threatening looks.

Wearing a toga as usual, Oswald strolled up to Gideon. The soon-to-be-profane parrot was on his shoulder. He paused long enough to ask, "Worried about her?" And as always, his voice was a bark, but pitched low enough not to disturb the tiger going lazily through his paces a few feet away.

Gideon kept his gaze on Maggie and held his own voice low. "What do you think?" he snapped.

"Touchy, touchy. Can't you see it? They'd never turn on her. She's too like them."

"What?" This time, Gideon spared a glance at the aristocratic ex-professor and caught a glimmer of the cool wisdom Maggie had credited him with in the old man's eyes.

"Instinct, man, instinct. It's how they react, just like her. She feels with them, and they know it. I've often thought Maggie stands in no danger from most living creatures." He snorted suddenly. "But you'll go on worrying, I know. I'm told love does that to a man." He strode off briskly, as if he had somewhere important to go.

Gideon looked after him for a moment, then returned his attention to the cage. He didn't really think, or breathe easily, until Maggie had led the huge tiger back to his own cage and put him inside it. Rajah was the last of the cats, and when Sarah, talking a mile a minute, hurried up to Maggie and led her away, Gideon didn't follow them.

Instead, he wandered back toward Maggie's wagon, brooding. Oswald seemed to understand her, he realized, and Tina as well. How many others? Had her quarry recognized the threat of her? Did he, too, understand that Maggie fit here only because she wanted to? Because, if so . . .

Of course he was worried, Gideon thought. How in hell could he *not* be worried? Lions and tigers, and a faceless murderer who'd killed at least once to protect himself.

Love. Oswald had said that love did this to a man, made him worry.

Awake all night, listening to Leo thrash about and mewl as he dreamed, Gideon had tried to get everything straight. Except that nothing got straight; it was all curves and angles. And this morning, when he'd seen Maggie—wearing faded jeans and a man's shirt, with her hair in a ponytail so that she looked about sixteen—something peculiar had happened to him. She'd seemed terrifyingly fragile, a little pale, her eyes wide and dark, and something lurched inside him with a force that was dizzying.

She wasn't reflecting, he'd realized. Like a curtain drawn over a sunny window, the light was cut off. He had watched her, seeing that she behaved as always with the carnies, her mood and attitude suited to theirs or their needs. It was only with him that she drew into herself. He knew it wasn't a new mood of hers, another color of the chameleon, or even his own inner struggles being mirrored back by her.

This was something else. And because of the change, he realized he was changing as well. Presented, not with a bright and multifaceted surface his mind had to puzzle but with a quiet, still surface that thought would never probe, his senses had reached out of their own volition. He stopped thinking about her because he was feeling about her.

He found himself at Maggie's wagon and sat down on the top step. "Hell of a thing to be doing at my age," he murmured to his faithful companion.

Leo put his paws on a step and rested his chin on Gideon's knee. "Wooo," he murmured in return.

Gideon scratched behind one ridiculous funnel-shaped ear. "She's gone dark, cat. She said she loved me—and then just closed a door somewhere. How do I get it open again?"

Leo lifted his head and chattered insistently and at considerable length.

Gideon was still a rational man, despite the strong new connection with his emotions. For the most part he believed in rational things. There was still a very large part of his logical mind that firmly maintained a human could not understand what a cat was saying even if a cat was saying anything sensible in the first place.

Which was highly debatable.

So, when during Leo's earnest monologue he realized what he had to do, he told himself it was simply a decision whose time had come. Inspiration, perhaps, or merely the new connections with his emotions. It had nothing to do with feline wisdom, of course. But when the cat went silent and looked at him expectantly, he patted him on the head nonetheless.

"Thanks, pal."

There was no harm, he thought, in leaving room for possibilities.

He waited throughout what became a very long day, watching Maggie, occasionally talking to her about casual things he thought neither of them paid attention to. She kept herself busy, helping

Sarah with a new clown costume for Lamont, spending a couple of hours with the three little boys working on their reading skills, mending a broken teapot that had Malcolm almost in tears.

And Gideon saw her relief when, after searching Jasper's wagon thoroughly, she and Lamont found a scribbled note underneath his pillow saying that he was going to visit family and would catch up with them later.

"It's his handwriting," she told Gideon quietly in passing. "I don't know, but at least it'll calm everyone down."

Gideon wasn't sure about the convenient note either, but knew there was nothing they could do except appear to accept it. At least for the time being.

He waited. He watched Maggie as she sat on the steps of her wagon brushing her long, pale hair dry after her shower that evening. He wanted to go to her, take the brush and do that for her. For him. But there were people around.

Always people around.

It was midnight when he crawled out of his tent to find Leo sitting up, funnel ears perked with interest. The camp was quiet, only the night sounds ruffling the silence. Moonlight spilled brightly, and he saw no sign of movement anywhere.

"Wooo?" Leo murmured.

"On the sleeping bag—not in it," Gideon responded absently, his attention fixed on Maggie's wagon. He held the opening until Leo scurried inside, then let it fall and went to the wagon. He knocked softly on the door.

"Maggie?"

There was silence.

"Maggie, I know you're not asleep."

After a moment there were quiet sounds, and a sliver of light appeared at the bottom of the door.

The sun was shining on the sea,
Shining with all his might:
He did his very best to make
The billows smooth and bright—
And this was odd, because it was
The middle of the night.

Seven

Gideon came into the wagon, closing the door behind him. The lamp by Maggie's bed was turned down low, but the room was so small that there seemed to be plenty of light. She was sitting up in bed, still under the covers, her knees drawn up and her arms wrapped loosely around them. He thought she was wearing just a T-shirt, probably oversize, which explained why she hadn't gotten up.

"It's late," she said.

He crossed the narrow space to the bed and sat down on the edge, looking at her steadily. "I hope it isn't too late. Do you love me, Maggie?"

Her lashes fluttered slightly, as if she would have looked away but couldn't somehow. "Yes."

"I don't believe you," he said softly.

Maggie had endured quite a lot, one way and another, but that simple statement did more to undermine her control than anything yet. She was in love and trying to be quiet about it, to keep herself from overwhelming Gideon with the sheer raw force of her emotions. And here he was with his shuttered eyes and stony expression, calling her a liar.

She couldn't deflect this, couldn't turn away from it and take the time to be calm. He wouldn't let her, and the pressure was building like something alive inside her.

Touch me . . . no, don't. Leave. But if you go, will you come back? I don't know what you want. . . . Is this what crazy really is? I don't like it much, at least not holding it inside. It hurts so inside. Don't make me let it out, it'll be worse when it's out, I couldn't bear it if I let it out and you didn't want it. . . .

"I can't help what you believe," she said shakily.

"Can't you?" His voice remained level. "I want to see it, Maggie. All you've done is say the words. Do you know what I think? I think the words are all you have. You're very good at reflecting emotion, I have to give you credit. Just like a mirror. And I'll admit I was fascinated. The kid in me, I suppose; every child is intrigued by mirrors. The wonder of imagining what might lie beyond the bright, reflective surface."

"Stop," she said.

He ignored her whisper. "I've grown up, Maggie. I know what the back side of a mirror looks like. It's dark and dull. No mystery. And a man doesn't want a reflection, in his life and in his bed. He wants a warm, loving woman, not the cold mirror image of one."

Nobody said it would hurt like this. Don't say anymore. Can't you see it? It isn't cold at all, it's hot . . . and it's truth . . . why won't you believe me? Why are you hurting me this way? Don't . . . please, don't . . .

"That's a neat trick of yours, sweetheart. The perfect woman—as long as a man doesn't reach too deep. Smiles when I want them. Anger when I feel like fighting. Passion on demand." His voice had taken on a cutting note.

"This isn't you," she murmured, hurt and puzzlement obscuring her thoughts as the pressure of emotions built steadily. "I don't understand why you're saying these things."

Gideon didn't know how long he could keep it up. Her eyes were so wide and dark they seemed bottomless, unlit, the door still closed. *Dammit,* what would it take? Grimly, he held on to his scornful tone.

"Why? I just wanted you to know that I understand now. It's all been a game, hasn't it? All the pretty reflections blinding me. You were the bait, weren't you, Maggie? The bait to keep Wonderland in business." He hoped desperately that he was right, that he'd found the key, because otherwise she'd never forgive him for making that accusation a second time.

Bait? Oh, no . . . Mirrors . . . I wish I hated you.

When it happened, it caught Gideon by surprise. He didn't know what he'd been expecting, couldn't know what to expect, really, but he recognized it nevertheless. It was the most mesmerizing thing he'd ever seen.

The eyes *were* windows to the soul. Maybe, after all, it was everyone else's eyes that were mirrors, not Maggie's. Because when the light came, it began so deeply within her it could have come from no other place. And there were no hints now, no vague ripples that might have been things moving in unseen depths; it was all there, all of her. Intelligence, mischief, temper, humor, fey wisdom, tolerance, passion . . . all the glances that spoke of mad things understood, and solemn looks and unconventional words and all the sweetness.

By the time the light reached the surface of her eyes—vividly green, iridescent—and blazed out at him, Gideon had found one thing more. He hadn't comprehended the sheer, raw fury of it, and there was a split second when he wanted to say, *Don't do that, don't love me that much*, but then it was all right, it was perfect, and he wanted it more than he wanted his next breath.

"Maggie," he whispered.

"Bait?" she snapped, her voice shaking with a lot more than hurt and bewilderment now. "I love you, you idiot!" She scrambled from under the covers and onto her knees, silvery hair flying around her as if her emotions were literally electric. The T-shirt did little to conceal her, and Gideon was so distracted he barely felt the small hands on his shoulders as she tried to shake him.

"How *dare* you say I'm just a reflection!"

Gideon followed his instincts. He yanked her completely against him, one hand tangling in her hair—and it felt alive, that silver silk, clinging to him—as he covered her angry lips with his own. Fists beat against his shoulders and back for a few seconds, then finally slowed. Her fingers uncurled and found their way into his hair as her mouth softened beneath his.

He eased her back onto the bed, still kissing her, leaning over her. His lips left hers finally and trailed over her face, discovering the salt of her tears.

"Don't," he said huskily. "Don't, Maggie."

"You hurt me," she whispered, wet green eyes looking up at him with childlike pain.

"I know. I'm sorry. But you'd shut me out, and I had to find a way in." He smoothed the tears away with his thumbs, surrounding her face with gentle hands. "At first I couldn't see anything but reflections—and then I couldn't see anything at all. You were hiding from me."

She bit her bottom lip. "I didn't want to, but I felt so much, and you didn't want it—"

"I do want it," he said in sudden fierceness. "I want your love. You said it was mine, and I want it."

Maggie felt her heart turn over with a bump, and she swallowed hard, hoping that what she saw in his face was real. "You don't think I'd be out of place in your world?"

He kissed her. "Honey, you'd be right at home anywhere, even on Mars."

In a conditioned reflex, because she felt so much it was frightening, her mind darted off on the tangent. "Mars? There aren't any people there; science disproved them. And the canals aren't really canals at all, they—"

Gideon kissed her again. "Why are you wandering off?"

She tried to catch her breath. Impossible; the word was in her vocabulary, after all. "To Mars? Because I had to look away for a minute."

Perhaps oddly, he understood. "You don't have to look away from us, Maggie. We're forever, remember?"

"Are you sure?" she whispered. "I couldn't bear it if you weren't sure. That's another reason I hid."

Gideon brushed a silvery strand of hair away

from her face, smiling. "I'm sure. I've loved you since the moment you turned around and looked at me, sweetheart. I just didn't have the sense to stop thinking and let myself feel."

Her smile was one he'd never seen before. "I've waited all my life for you. What kept you?"

Whimsically, he said, "I guess I had to fall through Alice's mirror before I could see through yours. And it's been a hell of a bumpy ride."

"That's what happens when you forget what every child knows," she said in a solemn tone. "The back side of a mirror isn't dark and dull at all—if you get there the right way."

"A lesson I'll never forget." He kissed her, the first gentle touch becoming something else when her response was instant and heated. "Maggie," he murmured against her lips, "it feels like I've waited for you all my life."

"No more waiting." Her arms tightened around his neck. "I love you, Gideon. I love you so much."

It really did feel as if he had waited for her forever, the tensions, frustrations, and desires of the past days almost exploding inside him. Knowing now that the woman in his arms had an infinite capacity to feel all that he felt, and to return it with the same ferocity, freed him. For the first time in his adult life he could relinquish his need to control.

It was a new and heady kind of freedom to just feel, to sate himself with an emotional and sensual awareness of another person so intense it was shattering. Emotionally, he already felt bonded to her, connected by some affinity his mind had at first blocked, as if it had always lain, unseen, inside him. And his senses opened up in a way he'd never felt, dazzling him with the burst of raw impulses. He had thought he'd known desire for her before, but this. . . .

At first, it was almost too much, a blind compulsion to hold her tightly against him, as if his very cells needed to merge with hers until they became one being. But they couldn't get close enough for that, and holding her wasn't enough, not nearly enough, to satisfy his terrible craving.

Maggie felt his hand touch her thigh, and then a tug at the hem of her shirt as he drew it up with slightly rough impatience. As driven as he was, she helped, pulling her arms from the sleeves when he lifted her a bit to get the shirt off. Her long hair caught in the neckline and was swept to one side, spilling over the pillow and the edge of the bed in a shower of silver as the shirt was tossed onto the floor.

"Maggie . . ."

It never occurred to her to be embarrassed or self-conscious because she was lying naked in his arms. And, if it had occurred to her, his expression would have banished those feelings instantly. He looked at her, she thought in wonder, as if she were the most beautiful woman he had ever seen. His gray gaze, burning almost silver, moved over her with such an intensity that it might have been his touch on her flesh. In response the glowing embers inside her burst into flame.

"It's . . . too much," she said breathlessly, the force of her own feelings overwhelming her. "I can't—"

"Yes, you can," he interrupted, his voice raw and hoarse. He kissed her, insistently this time, demanding that she hold nothing back. "It's mine. All of that primitive emotion was meant for me, and I want it."

She never doubted that he understood, that he saw or felt or sensed the wildness inside her. But he wasn't drawing away from it—he was urging her to let go, to free the feelings and share them with him. And for the first time in her life, she couldn't look away from them herself. With a sound almost like a sob, she reached for his shirt, helping him to discard the barriers that kept them apart.

She hadn't realized he would be so beautiful. Muscles rippled powerfully under tanned flesh as he moved, his strength vividly revealed now. The mat of red-gold hair covering his broad chest was soft and springy under her fingers, the hard planes and angles of his body so compellingly different from her own that he seemed alien, yet stirringly familiar as well. And all her emotions swirled wildly around an aching emptiness.

"Dear Lord, Maggie," he murmured, one hand sliding up over her ribcage to surround a firm breast, "I need you so badly."

She gasped when his mouth closed hotly over her tight nipple, the sensation so stark it was almost painful. Her fingers twined in his thick hair and a soft moan escaped her throat. He was burning her, setting all her nerves on fire as his mouth moved on her. The hunger in him shuddered through his powerful body and awoke answering tremors in her body. Hot shivers broke like waves over her.

The empty ache inside her seemed to pulse, throb, growing moment by moment until she couldn't be still, couldn't breathe except in shallow gasps, and couldn't keep the sounds locked in her throat. She felt his hand slide down over her belly, warm and heavy, and she was opening to him eagerly, an instinctive tension holding her poised on the brink of something because he was so close to the awful emptiness.

She cried out almost silently when he touched her, her feverish body arching helplessly. His probing, stroking fingers intensified the ache until she thought she'd go mad, until that emptiness was all she could feel and it was consuming her.

His name burst from her in a sound that was love and need and desperation, a sound winging free of her because it belonged to him now. It was a sound he felt pierce him and touch an answering chord deep inside him.

With a rough sound of his own, he spread her legs and slipped between them, willing the last threads of his control to hold steady just a little longer. But Maggie's need was impatient of control, and she surged upward to meet him, possessing him as surely as he possessed her. Her body accepted him, claimed him, as if the certainty of him as her one and only love was stamped in her very cells.

Gideon felt that certainty as well, felt it in the fire consuming them both, in the tight clasp of her body, in the shattering culmination that hurled them over the rim of something so imperative that he knew it had been intended.

In that stark moment of wild physical pleasure and profound emotion, he understood. He belonged to Maggie, not in any possessive sense, but in truth. More basic than any of society's conventional tags—friend, lover, wife—she was his mate.

For life.

"Wooooo?"

Maggie yawned and snuggled closer to Gideon's

side, wondering vaguely what that peculiar noise was.

"Wooooooo?"

She felt his arms tighten around her and was conscious of a drowsy surge of delight. How nice, sleeping with a man. This particular man. Every inch of her body was tingling warmly. Somebody should have told her. She would have gone to San Francisco and hunted this man down years ago.

"Woo-oooo?"

"Tell him to go away," Gideon muttered, pulling her an impossible inch nearer.

Maggie yawned again. One completely sleepless night and one virtually sleepless night had taken their toll. She thought she could possibly move if somebody lit a fire under her, otherwise it was a lost cause.

"Woooo!"

"Sweetheart, if you love me, strangle that cat," Gideon said, sounding as plaintive as the feline outside.

"He loves you too," she murmured. "You abandoned him last night."

"It's his own fault. He told me to." Forcing his eyes open, Gideon found that she had lifted her head from his shoulder and was looking at him in mild puzzlement. A brief and rather uncertain laugh escaped him. "Never mind. It sounds just as crazy on this side of the mirror."

Maggie accepted that amiably. "What time is it?"

He looked at his wrist. "I don't know. My watch is gone." Peering past her, he added, "It's right on the table there. On your side."

The bed wasn't all that big. Maggie roused herself enough to reach around behind her until she found the table and then his watch. She stared at the thing for a minute, then sighed heavily. "It's after eight. I hope Farley fed the animals."

"Wooo," Leo commented miserably from the other side of the closed door.

"He wants in," Maggie said.

"He isn't coming in. And we're not going out. Do you hear that, Leo?" Gideon demanded, raising his voice slightly. "Go away. Mind your own business."

"Why aren't we going out?" she asked interestedly. "Not that I can move at the moment, but we have to eat."

"I want you all to myself for a while. It's an interesting world, your side of the mirror . . . but crowded."

Quite suddenly, Maggie sat up. "I just remembered. Today it won't be crowded. One day a week almost everybody goes into town to shop and maybe see a movie. At least one of us usually offers to stay and watch the camp. If you and I stay—"

"That sounds—"

"—we can look for the cache," she finished.

Gideon closed his eyes briefly, then hauled her back down to his side. "I have another suggestion. Let's go to San Francisco. Richmond. Australia."

Maggie folded her hands on his broad chest and rested her chin on them. "Anyplace but here?"

"That's the idea."

Gravely, she said, "I have to finish what I started, Gideon. I owe it to my family. It shouldn't take much longer. If I know my uncle Cyrus, he'll find the information we need. Then all that's left is to find the cache and get a confession."

He stared at her. "That's all? Honey, we might—

just might—find the cache. If it exists, that is. We might even find out who the guilty party is. But how on earth do you expect to get a confession? And why? The goods would probably convict him."

"Not of murder."

Gideon wasn't surprised. He'd had a hollow feeling she was going to say just that. And since he understood her, since he could, now, see the determination in her eyes, he knew it was useless to argue. But, naturally, he tried.

"Maggie, you said yourself there was no evidence. That the police ruled the death as accidental. No murderer in his right mind would confess to—" he stopped, blinked. "Is anybody here in their right mind? Other than me and thee, that is?"

Brushing the question aside, she said, "A confession might be a problem. What we need is evidence. Or a witness. I have to be able to make the killer think I know *exactly* what went on the night Merlin was killed."

"And make yourself a target?"

"Of course not. I wasn't here when Merlin was killed—how could I know? Obviously, somebody told me. Which means that someone else knows the truth. So why would the killer want to get rid of me? It wouldn't help him."

"What if he doesn't work all that out, Maggie? He may be an impulse killer; maybe that was why Merlin was just pushed into a well instead of being done in by a method that was a little more fancy."

"You'll be near," she said dismissively. "Out of sight, though. He'll talk to me, I think, but not if he knows anyone else is listening. I have a pocket recorder with a very good microphone, so we can get it on tape."

"We both keep saying he. At least tell me if any of the women are suspects."

"Well, none of them has been here less than seven years. Except me, of course."

"So it's Lamont—and somebody else?"

Maggie frowned at him. "I was wondering if you'd remember that, dammit."

"I have an excellent memory. You said that Lamont had joined Wonderland a couple of years ago when it passed through his town. Which town was that, by the way?"

"Dallas. And it was three years ago, according to the account books. Would you care to guess who our other suspect is?"

Without hesitation Gideon said, "Farley."

"Why him?"

"I don't like him."

Maggie raised her head and gazed down at him. "That was a gut response, wasn't it?"

He thought about it for a moment. "I suppose so. Logically, he's a good suspect—and there aren't many. I mean, think about it. To consider Malcolm or Oswald is laughable; underneath their poses, they're two old men enjoying themselves."

"Astute of you," Maggie said, watching him.

Gideon continued to pursue suspects. "Tom and Sarah—no way. He'd kill to protect her, but he strikes me as a good man. She couldn't do it, period. Buster's parents seem the most sensible of the lot, but also the most content; I don't think they want any more than they've got."

"And Tina?"

"She could kill—for the right reasons. I don't think money would do it, though." Gideon was silent for a moment, then said, "Maggie, what about Jasper?"

"He's been with Wonderland more than twenty years."

"Okay. But what if that's the beauty of it? Suppose Jasper went off to visit family sometime during the past few years and committed a robbery?"

"Damn. That never occurred to me."

"You've all said he wandered off occasionally. And no one seemed surprised to find the note that said he was visiting relatives now. Suppose he lit out and took the cache?"

"I'd almost prefer that answer to the one that's been haunting me," Maggie said seriously.

"That he's dead?"

"Yes. But Gideon, if Jasper's the killer and he's left for good—who's been watching you?"

"Maybe I imagined it. God knows this place is conducive to lunatic thoughts. In fact, this whole thing is so bizarre, I don't know what to think."

She smiled at him. "You're not as bewildered as you say you are; you've got the people here summed up rather neatly. In fact, you'd make a good detective."

"Perish the thought." Gideon sighed. "Tell me something. Are you often involved in this kind of thing?"

"Well, not murder, naturally. And my family doesn't get into trouble that often."

"I knew I should have worried more about your family," he murmured wryly.

"You'll love them, I promise." She reflected, then added honestly, "Once you get used to them, that is."

He lifted his head and kissed her. "I love a mad angel. I suppose there are worse fates."

"Of course there are. I love a banker."

Gideon slid his hand down to one rounded hip and swatted her lightly. "Don't say nasty things about our future livelihood. Though, I must admit, the office is going to seem very dull after Wonderland."

"I'll visit every day and bring your lunch."

"I'll look forward to that." He kissed her again and murmured, "There's no lock on that door, is there?"

"No one's going to disturb us unless it's an emergency."

"If anyone disturbs us, there will be an emergency."

When they emerged from the wagon around ten, they found Leo sulking, the other animals snoozing peacefully, and the human inhabitants of the camp grouped near Tina's wagon apparently engaged in an acrimonious discussion.

"I think I'll go shave," Gideon said, eyeing the group while he tried to imagine what kinds of questions he'd be confronted with after having spent the night in Maggie's wagon.

"Coward." She grinned up at him. "But all to the good, I suppose. I'll go over there looking dreamy eyed and tell them you and I will stay here today. We want to be alone," she added soulfully.

Gideon, understanding the depths of her emotions as no one else ever would, wasn't disturbed by her mockery. "You do that," he told her politely. He tipped her chin up and kissed her.

"Wooo?"

He looked over his shoulder at the cat, who'd been slinking along in his shadow looking sulky and muttering to himself. "Come on, cat, and you can watch me shave. I realize that isn't entertain-

ment of the first order, but you seemed to enjoy it
yesterday."

Unrelenting, Leo snorted, but followed nonetheless as his fallen idol started across the camp.

Maggie looked after them for a moment, then
let a few of her emotions float to the surface as
she went over to the group near Tina's wagon.
"Good morning," she told them.

Farley cocked an eye up at the sun. "Barely," he
conceded.

" 'Tis love that makes the world go round,"
Oswald murmured, then added a hasty, "Hush!"
when the parrot on his shoulder began the first
few bars of what sounded like a sailor's ditty.

Lamont, who was wearing a bright blue nose
that looked rather like a bird's perch, said simply,
"Well, I like him."

"The parrot?" Maggie questioned, lost for once.

"No. Gideon. He's nice."

Tina grinned faintly. "As long as he doesn't
snore."

Maggie strove to look dignified. "If he did, I
didn't notice. Now, why're you all standing here?"

"Deciding who stays," Tina told her.

"No problem. Gideon and I will." Rather to her
surprise, Maggie felt herself blushing slightly. "We
wouldn't mind a little time alone."

Sean looked up at her, faintly puzzled. "I thought
you was with him in your wagon. Was somebody
else in there too?"

Maggie looked somewhat helplessly at Tina, who
said instantly, "Go in and put your shoes on,
Sean. You're not going to town barefoot."

"Why not?" the boy demanded.

"They won't let you in the movie."

The threat effectively distracted Sean, and he darted into the wagon without delay.

"Thanks," Maggie murmured.

"Don't mention it." Tina grinned again. "Your time will come. Kids always ask the most awkward questions."

"I've noticed. Tina, the rent for the field's due; on the way to town, can you stop at Mr. Davis's and pay him?"

"Sure. Oh—and I've left some snacks in the wagon for whoever we elected to stay. In case you and Gideon get hungry. We'll eat in town."

Maggie nodded, then looked at the others questioningly. "Do we need any supplies I don't know about?"

"We could use fresh meat for the cats," Farley said. "That means I'd better take along the battery for the ice locker and get it recharged."

"All right, I'll get the money. You all had better hurry if you want to have time to shop, eat, and see a movie." They all scattered while Maggie went to get the money box from its hiding place in the floor of the boa's cage.

Around half an hour later, the supply wagon had been unloaded of its remaining supplies to make room for more, and it and the only other "light" wagon—not one of the huge antiques that were so cumbersome—were hitched to teams. The carnies claimed their places, and the two wagons rolled out of the field and onto the road.

Gideon, standing beside Maggie as they watched the others depart, couldn't help but think that the little procession looked both ridiculous and curiously charming.

"Won't they get stared at?" he asked Maggie.

"No, not really. We had to get a special permit to

drive the wagons through town, and the first couple of visits we attracted a lot of attention, but we've been here for weeks now, and everybody's pretty much used to us."

He looked down at her, smiling slightly. "You always say *us* when you talk about this place."

"One of the tricks to blending in is to consider yourself a part of what's around you."

"I see." Gideon put his arms around her and pulled her close. "So, what are you now?"

"Carny," she said innocently.

He rested his forehead against hers and sighed.

Maggie giggled, but then sobered. "You know, I've had a happy life, but I've never felt this alive before. The whole world looks different, brighter and filled with promise. Because of you. I love you, Gideon."

"I love you too, sweetheart." He kissed her, then uttered a mild oath. "The first time we've been completely alone here, and you want to go treasure hunting."

"Think of it this way," she said consolingly. "The sooner we find what we need to find, the sooner we can leave."

He brightened. "Is that a promise?"

"Cross my heart."

"All right, then, dammit. Are we going to ransack the wagons?"

"Gently ransack. We don't want anyone to know we've been searching. And the wagons are most likely; it's a little tricky to hide something in a tent."

"Okay. Who first?"

Maggie sent a speculative glance over the encampment. "I don't know that it matters. I have a feeling that wherever the cache is, it won't be anywhere near the person who stole it. He'd be cautious, and he'd assume there was always the off chance that it might be found."

"Jasper's wagon is empty," Gideon noted, "but you searched it yesterday."

"And didn't see a thing out of place. We'll save him for last, I think."

Gideon nodded and looked thoughtful. "All the other wagons are occupied. If I were going to hide something in someone else's wagon, I'd pick the person least observant, and least likely to explore the nooks and crannies." He frowned suddenly. "Did Merlin have a wagon?"

Maggie's eyes widened. "How stupid of me! He did have a wagon. When he was killed, Farley and Lamont drew straws because they both wanted a wagon. Lamont won."

"Then let's start there."

Leo accompanied them as far as the wagon, but then, apparently recalling his exclusion from Maggie's wagon before and not expecting an invitation into this one, he elected to sprawl in the shade underneath it. He was no longer sulky, but appeared resigned rather than delighted.

Since the carnies only shut their doors at night or when they wanted privacy, the door of Lamont's wagon was standing open.

"At least we don't have to pick a lock," Gideon said wryly.

"It does feel like breaking and entering, doesn't it?" Maggie climbed the steps ahead of Gideon and went inside. "I'm glad he has a window; we won't have to light the lamp to see what we're doing."

Gideon stood gazing around. As in all the wagons, there was little space. A daybed was against one wall below the single high window, and it was covered with a colorful patchwork quilt of some artistry; there was an overstuffed easy chair upholstered in scarlet velvet worn thin in a number of places; a small wooden table on which sat an oil lamp; a scarred pine bureau; and finally, a card table set up along the wall with a round mirror hanging over it. The table was covered with jars, brushes, three wigs on stands, and a tray of grease pencils, which also held the new noses Gideon had provided so recently.

In a distracted tone as she looked around thoughtfully, Maggie said, "All of Merlin's things were shipped to Uncle Cyrus. Balthazar sent them."

"Your uncle's last name isn't Durant, is it? I mean, if Balthazar knew that—"

"No, it's Cyrus Fortune. Merlin's was Lewis."

Gideon nodded. "You realize that we don't even know what we're looking for?"

"I do realize that, yes." Maggie sat down on the bed, frowning. "If I were something valuable, where would I be?" she murmured almost to herself.

"You are something priceless."

She flashed him a quick smile. "Concentrate, please, on the matter at hand."

"If you insist. Something valuable. Something portable. Something easily hidden." He looked slowly around the wagon. "Gold is heavy. Artworks tend to be too big to be easily hidden. Jewels, maybe. Paper money or the equivalent."

"The equivalent?"

"Stock certificates, bonds, certificates of deposit, things like that."

Maggie nodded, then said slowly, "Merlin must have found something. But even if he did, how would he know who the guilty party was? If you find something hidden in your wagon, would you automatically assume it was stolen? And if so, and if you're an honest man, wouldn't you just go to the owner of the carnival and say look what I found?"

"You're sure Balthazar was clean?"

"Uncle Cyrus vouched for him. He was clean."

"Your uncle's name keeps popping up in this," Gideon observed mildly.

She smiled slightly. "He has a way of knowing things. In fact, I have a sneaking suspicion that he knows very well who killed Merlin."

"Then why on earth put you through this?"

"His own reasons. Maybe because he couldn't prove it and knows I'll do my best to. Or maybe . . ." Her voice trailed off as she looked at Gideon, and her eyes widened.

"Maybe what?"

She started laughing. "If he did . . . and I never suspected a thing . . . of all the sneaky—"

"Maggie, what are you talking about?"

Sobering finally, she cleared her throat and said, "I think we've been set up."

"By your uncle?"

"Uh-huh. I've seen him work, Gideon, he's really amazing. And he's been doing it as long as I can remember. My father used to say that if Uncle Cyrus had found a different outlet for his talents, he could have ruled the world."

Gideon took a step and sat down on the bed beside her. "Honey, what are you talking about? What talents?"

"Matchmaking talents. Oh, not just simple introductions between people, that's too easy. Uncle Cyrus arranges things so that two unsuspecting people encounter each other at precisely the right moment. If needed, he steps in at some point to help resolve the occasional problem. But I know of some people who never saw him or knew anything about his intervention and still owed their happiness to him."

After a moment Gideon said, "A few days ago I would have said—you have to be kidding. Now I'm willing to accept the possibility. But how could he know that Balthazar would be killed and leave me the carnival? That's why I came here."

A sudden gleam of amusement lit her vivid eyes. "Gideon, I'm surprised at you. Gored by a rhinoceros? That's the most lunatic thing I've ever heard."

"It takes nerve for you to say that to me," he said, an answering gleam in his own eyes.

She giggled. "Well, it is. I thought the whole thing was faked as soon as we got the announcement from the attorneys. I assumed Uncle Cyrus bought the carnival from Balthazar and had him ask me to take over while he dashed off into the sunset. It got me inside here, and everyone accepted it."

"Then why fabricate a will and— Oh. To get me here? Matchmaking?"

"It looks that way now. At the time I just assumed Uncle Cyrus had decided he didn't want a carnival, and I'd still have time until probate. I should have known better."

"It seems awfully elaborate."

Maggie nodded. "Definitely. His plans always are. Tell me, did you happen to inherit a 1958 black Caddie?"

"No, it wasn't mentioned in the will."

"Then that clinches it. Balthazar is very much alive, and probably sunning himself on some island. According to the carnies here who've known him longest, he loved that car like a child. Nobody could ever make me believe that he provided for Wonderland in a will and left his baby rusting away in a dockside parking lot somewhere."

Gideon stared at her for a moment, then said, "I don't know whether to thank your uncle or punch him in the nose."

She smiled. "He'll never admit to it. If either of us pinned him to the wall and demanded the truth, he'd widen his eyes—and you have no idea how innocent that sly old man can look—and say that the hand of man doesn't guide lovers, destiny does."

"He'd say that."

"Verbatim."

"And mean it?"

"Sure. But I decided when I was ten that destiny lived in the shape of my uncle Cyrus."

*"It's a poor sort of memory that only works
backwards," the Queen remarked.*

Eight

"He looked more like Colonel Sanders to me," Gideon said consideringly. "Of course, I only had a glimpse of him."

Maggie laughed, but shook her head. "Wait until you know him better. Look, knowing Uncle Cyrus, he won't help us out until he's good and ready, so we're on our own. If you were something valuable hidden in here, where would you be?"

"If I don't know what I am, how can I know where I am?" Gideon held up a hand when she frowned at him. "Okay, okay. I was hidden here when Merlin lived here, presumably. He found me—or some part of me. He wasn't looking for me, so he must have been doing something else. Moving something, maybe?"

Slowly, she said, "The thing in here least likely to be moved is the daybed; it takes up too much space anywhere except against this wall."

"Then let's try it."

They got up, each of them going to an end of the bed. It wasn't unreasonably heavy, but the lack of space in the wagon made it awkward to move. Still, they were able to shift it about two feet out from its wall.

Maggie knelt down on her side and looked carefully. "A piece of the paneling seems a little scarred. Do you have a penknife?"

"No, but—" He squeezed over to Lamont's makeup table and found what looked like a putty knife, then managed to get around the bed to Maggie's side and sat down on the edge as he handed her the knife. "Try this."

There was a horizontal seam on one section of the paneling about twelve inches up from the floor, and she picked at it carefully with the knife. The two edges of wood had been tacked down, but a few minutes work loosened the two tacks on the upper section. Maggie eased the knife blade into the seam, letting the blade slide upward, and then pulled steadily.

The tacks came out, the rattle as they struck the floor loud in the silence. She wedged her fingers into the gap and pulled harder, until the section of paneling above the seam gave way completely. A manila envelope, its straining sides bound haphazardly with black electrician's tape, slid out and hit the floor with a thump.

"I'll be damned," Gideon said.

Maggie sat back on her heels, holding the package, and looked up at him. "Maybe we should hang out a shingle."

"It could just be somebody's old love letters, you know."

"I bet you say 'bah, humbug' at Christmas too," she said, carefully opening one end of the envelope.

"I'm a realist," he said firmly.

She peered into the envelope, then drew out a

sheet of paper, studied it briefly, and handed it to him. "Better check your definition of reality."

He stared at the embossed page in his hand. "Bearer bonds. Good Lord, how much is here?"

Maggie had pulled the remaining pages from the tattered envelope and looked through them rapidly. "It looks like about two million dollars' worth. Enough to kill for."

"Yes . . ."

"What is it?" There was a peculiar note in his voice, and it alerted her.

Slowly, Gideon said, "I'm beginning to believe your uncle might just be destiny—because I don't believe in the long arm of coincidence. The company that issued these bonds was looking for expansion money about four years ago."

"A company in San Francisco?"

"Yes, and they came to my bank. I spent several days at their offices, going over their plans. A week before the deal was due to be finalized, there was a robbery. Two point three million in bearer bonds just waltzed out the front door; it was an inside job."

Maggie waited silently, watching him.

"The employee had faked all his identification well enough to get by their security checks—minor ones, at his level. He worked there a few months, made friends with the guard at the vault. And then one day he doped the guard's morning coffee and somehow got the vault open. He vanished like smoke. They never found him."

"Did you see him there?" Maggie asked. "Before the robbery, while you were working at their offices?"

Gideon shook his head slightly. "It was a big company with a lot of employees. He'd had a photo taken because it was company policy and the newspapers ran it later. I might have glanced at it then. Hell, I could have seen him a dozen times while I was at the offices and never really looked at him."

"Don't think about him there," she said. "He probably doesn't look like that now. Think of the people here. One at a time. Just the faces. The eyes. The way they move."

He went still suddenly, his gaze fixed on the wall. Then he looked at Maggie, the connection made in his mind. "Damn. I did see him there. He brought me some files at least twice. But he wasn't wearing a kilt. Or a garland of flowers in his hair."

Sighing softly, Maggie said, "I never really believed it could be Lamont. So it had to be Farley. No wonder you've been a threat to him. He knew you could remember. No one else could have connected him with a theft in San Francisco. He joined Wonderland in Little Rock."

"I'm sorry, Maggie."

"So am I." She smiled. "It would be easier if he seemed more of a villainous kind of person."

Gideon was silent for a moment, then said, "The police can definitely get a conviction on the theft. It'll put him away for a long time, honey."

She knew what he was saying, but shook her head. "He killed Merlin. He has to pay for that too. If only—if only someone could tell me at least part of what happened that night, enough to convince him someone had seen or heard—"

"Maggie?" She looked startled, he thought, as if something had suddenly occurred to her.

"Bear pond," she murmured. "Someone named Merlin found a bear pond."

"What Sean told me? Bear pond . . ." Then he realized, and it made perfect sense once you thought like a six-yearold. "Of course. *Bearer bond.* Merlin found a bearer bond."

"He heard it and didn't understand. So he turned it around until it made some kind of sense to him. Gideon, Sean's our witness. You said it yourself, he sees and hears everything around here. Even what he isn't supposed to. Even what he doesn't understand."

"Will the police believe a six-year-old?"

Maggie frowned. "Maybe they won't have to, If Sean can tell me enough of what happened that night, I might be able to convince Farley there was a witness without telling him who it was."

"It's dangerous, Maggie."

She looked up at him steadily. "I don't think Farley would hurt me. But we'll set it up carefully, just to be on the safe side. You'll be near. And then it'll be over."

He leaned forward, elbows on his knees, and said, "I can't talk you out of this, can I?"

"You probably could," she admitted. "But I'm asking you not to try. I need to do this, Gideon."

"All right. What first?"

"First," she said, getting to her feet, "we put this bed back where it belongs. Then we get a bottle of wine and those snacks Tina left for us and go back to my wagon. Until the others return late this afternoon, there really isn't much for us to do. Except enjoy the time alone."

"You're just trying to take my mind off this," he said.

"Will it work, do you think?"

"Let's find out."

It worked.

It was after five when the carnies returned to the encampment, and the quiet was broken by the natural conversation, laughter, and squabbles of people who had spent the day enjoying themselves. The teams were unhitched, supplies and individual purchases sorted and put away, and everyone began to settle down.

Maggie had no difficulty in speaking to Sean alone, because he wanted to tell her all about the movie he'd seen in town. She sat on the steps of her wagon talking to him awhile. Nearby, Gideon took down his barely used tent—with the enthusiastic help of Leo, who'd finally cheered up—and kept an unobtrusive eye out to make sure no one overheard what Sean had to say.

Smiling, Maggie listened as the boy minutely described the movie, whose special effects had won his admiration. When he finally ran out of wows, she spoke to him in a careful tone that was serious without being at all threatening.

"Sean, I need to talk to you about something very important."

"What?"

Understanding children, Maggie knew that she'd never get anything out of Sean until he was certain he wouldn't be punished for having been where he shouldn't have been. She also knew that Sean loved secrets.

"It's a secret," she said gravely.

His eyes brightened.

"The thing is, I only know part of the secret, and I think you know part of it too. I think that one night when you were supposed to be in bed, you sneaked outside."

"Ma won't let me do that," he said innocently.

"This time," Maggie said sincerely, "she's going to be proud of you for doing it. Because you discovered a secret. And you were smart enough not to tell anybody about it."

His brow furrowed. "What secret did I find, Maggie?"

"You found out that Merlin had found a bear pond, didn't you?"

Sean studied a grubby thumb for a moment, then looked at her from underneath his lashes. "Ma won't be mad at me?"

"I promise. When you and I put our heads together and figure out all of the secret, your ma will be very proud of you."

After a moment he said with a slight air of grievance, "Well, I didn't actually *see* the bear pond. I just heard Farley and Merlin talkin' about it."

"When was that, Sean?"

"It was the night before. You know. Before Merlin fell into the well. Farley was mad."

Since the well where Merlin had been found had been some distance from the encampment, and since the children hadn't been told what had happened to him, Sean's knowledge of that looked promising. Unless, of course, he had simply overheard some of the adults discussing what had happened.

"Why is it a secret?" he asked Maggie. "Because Merlin fell into the well?"

"Let's see if we can figure it out," she said seriously. "I want you to tell me exactly what you saw and heard that night. Take your time, and think about it, all right?"

"Sure. Ma went to bed early, so I sneaked out . . ."

It was some minutes later before Sean finished

his story. Maggie asked a few questions and then extracted a very important promise from the boy before he raced off toward Tina's wagon.

Maggie reached into the pocket of her skirt briefly, then got up and went over to Gideon, who was staring down at a rather lumpy-looking heap of canvas on the ground. "Did you get enough?" he asked casually.

She answered in the same tone. "More than I expected to. And I got it on tape." She patted her pocket.

"Wooo?" the lump of canvas said mournfully.

"What have you done to Leo?" Maggie asked.

"I folded him up in the tent."

"Deliberately?"

Gideon looked at her, mildly shocked. "Would I do that? To a defenseless creature?"

"No, but we're talking about Leo."

He returned his gaze to the canvas, which was now twitching urgently. "I don't suppose I could tie the whole thing up with twine and send it back to the store?"

"Better not."

"Wooo?"

"It's not that I have anything against cats in general; and Leo in particular," Gideon explained. "It's just that he keeps saying things I think I understand. Unnerving."

"What did he say?"

"First he asked if I had a balcony in San Francisco, and then he criticized my tent-folding. So I folded him up in it. Maggie, if he'd been a Cheshire cat, I might have been able to handle it. But no. Your Wonderland had to have Leo."

"Do admit he's interesting."

"Woo-ooo?"

"He's weird. When he makes that noise, it just sounds pathetic; but when he chatters, it's like listening to a foreign language and reading the subtitles at the same time."

Leo began chattering. He sounded profane.

"We'd better get him out of there," Maggie said. "I haven't heard words like that since his tail got caught when he was trying to get into the bird cage."

Sighing, Gideon knelt down and began to unfold Leo. In an altered and lower voice he said, "We'll have to shut him in your wagon in the morning. Will he keep quiet?"

"If you tell him to."

Freed at last, Leo chattered briefly, ears flattened, and then stalked off toward Tina's wagon and his supper.

Gideon rose to his feet. "I've been royally told off," he noted, then slipped his arms around Maggie, glanced around at the archaic and slightly mad trappings of Wonderland, and looked at her somewhat ruefully. "I suppose all your very strange family will come to the wedding?"

"My family loves weddings," she said matter-of-factly. "And they bring interesting presents. Mother still talks about the urn she got from Aunt Zelda."

By now, Gideon recognized the detour her mind took around intense emotions, and he followed obediently. "What's so unusual about an urn?"

"Uncle Rudy was in it."

Gideon couldn't help but laugh. "He came for the wedding and just stayed, huh?"

"Well, no. Mother persuaded Aunt Zelda to take him back home again. He went in a pickle jar."

After struggling for a moment Gideon said, "How can you say things like that with a straight face?"

"Practice," she said, and chuckled.

Gideon hugged her hard. "You have to marry me," he told her fiercely. "We're forever."

Maggie slipped her arms up around his neck, her eyes open, for him, all the way to her soul. "I know we are. And I'll marry you just as soon as we can get Cousin Raynor back from France."

He followed the detour again. "Who's Cousin Raynor?"

"Our minister. He's been marrying the family for fifty years. It wouldn't be valid without Cousin Raynor."

Gideon kissed her. "Then, by all means, we'll have Cousin Raynor. And all the rest of them. How many *are* there?"

"Lots," she said happily

"I can hardly wait," Gideon told her, and wasn't at all surprised that it was nothing less than the truth.

It was barely dawn the next morning when Maggie, sitting on the steps of the supply wagon, saw Farley emerge from his tent and start toward her. Behind her and hidden in the darkness of the wagon, she knew that Gideon had seen as well—and that he was turning on the small recorder that had so accurately captured Sean's story the day before.

She saw Farley's cheerful smile, then watched it fade as he got near enough to see the manila envelope resting on her lap.

The camp was quiet, the animals not yet demanding their breakfasts, and Maggie kept her voice soft. "Good morning, Farley."

He came slowly toward her, kilted as always but

pale now. When he reached the feed barrels lined up near the steps, he stopped and leaned back against one of them, looking at her steadily. "I have a feeling it isn't going to be so good," he said quietly, the rhythm of Scotland gone from his voice. "What have you got there, Maggie?"

She rested her forearms on the envelope and gazed at him, feeling sad and disappointed because she had liked him. "I have over two million in negotiable bearer bonds. And I have all the answers I came here for."

"Answers?"

"Merlin was my cousin, Farley. I came here to find out what happened to him."

He laughed soundlessly. "I knew you were trouble from the first day. I just couldn't figure you out."

Maggie kept her voice even. "You stole these bonds from a company in California and got as far as Little Rock, where you joined the carnival. The first chance you had, you found a hiding place for the bonds in Merlin's wagon. And then everything went fine for nearly four years. But Merlin found one of the bonds, didn't he?"

"I don't know what you're talking about," Farley said.

"Sure, you do. But there's something you don't know. There was a witness, Farley. Someone who saw Merlin down on his knees beside the daybed, holding one of the bonds. I suppose he'd moved the bed because his rabbit had gotten behind it; I remember he always kept the rabbit with him.

"The bonds were hidden in this worn envelope; one of them probably just slipped out. You should have tacked down the paneling the first time instead of later. Somebody saw you tack it down later, after Merlin was killed.

"But that night there weren't any tacks. A bond slipped out. Merlin found it, and when he looked up, you were standing on the steps. And he told you, in surprise, that he'd found a bearer bond."

Farley was even more pale. "You weren't here then," he said harshly. "You couldn't have seen a thing. Who did?"

"Do you really think I'd tell you that? You've already killed once to protect yourself."

"It was an accident!" Farley burst out. "A stupid accident. The old man slipped when I grabbed for the bond. I didn't even know the well was there."

"Why did you take him out away from the camp if you didn't mean to kill him?" Maggie said flatly.

"I just wanted to talk to him, I swear. To split the money with him if he'd promise to keep his mouth shut. I'd waited nearly four years, Maggie. *Four years.* He said it was wrong, immoral, and that he was going to the police. But I'm no killer, not even for millions. I thought I'd grab the bond he was holding, because the statute of limitations wasn't up and the police could trace it back to San Francisco; they'd know too much about me then. I'd grab the bond and then run back and get the rest; he was an old man, I'd have a head start. It was a chance, and after four years I had to take it.

"But he slipped. And the well was only covered by a rotting piece of plywood. It happened so fast."

After a moment Maggie said, "You stayed with the carnival and kept quiet."

"What choice did I have?" Farley's voice was jerky. "I knew they wouldn't find him right away; by the time they did, the tracks would be gone—it started raining that night. I had to be with the carnival when they found him, or I'd have been suspected. The police called it an accident."

"And you thought you were safe again."

"I thought so. But then you came, and things started falling apart. Balthazar left. Everyone was tense about Merlin—I knew they wondered about the accident. Then Hughes came, and Jasper picked the worst moment to wander off to visit relatives. You thought something had happened to him, I could tell. Hughes thought so too."

Maggie was relieved to hear that Jasper's note had been genuine, but kept her mind on the matter at hand. "Gideon saw you at that company in San Francisco, didn't he? That's why you've stayed out of his way here, why you watched him all the time. You were afraid he'd recognize you."

Dully, Farley said, "He did, didn't he?"

"Yes."

Farley nodded. "I knew he would. Eventually. You can come out now, Gideon," he added in the same flat tone. "I might not be sure of much, but I know damned well you'd never let her risk herself needlessly."

Gideon appeared silently in the doorway behind Maggie, and when Farley saw the recorder in his hand, he grimaced faintly.

"Well, that's it, I guess. Like I said, I'm no killer. And I doubt you two are going to let me take the bonds and leave."

"Afraid not," Gideon said quietly.

Farley nodded. "Then do you mind if we go to the police right now? I'd rather not stick around and face everyone here."

Small-town police cope with most of the things their big-city brethren face; the major difference between them is that in small towns the officers usually have time to catch their breath and play a hand or two of poker between crimes. Another difference is that life in a small town moves at a slower pace, and most everybody knows everybody else, so things get straightened out with a minimum of fuss and an occasional gentle bit of blackmail.

"Now, George, we know you wouldn't want your missus knowing about those trips into Wichita to visit your lady friend, so you just tell us now why your store burned down before we have to start inquiring into how much it costs to keep an apartment in Wichita."

Since they deal with crises on a regular basis, police officers are not easily confused or rattled. They are also quite human in their masculine appreciation of feminine beauty. Which is why the four men in the police station jumped to their feet and beamed when Maggie walked in.

The confusion set in approximately three seconds later.

Since Maggie was upset about Farley, her mind darted from time to time as she explained why they were there, and the officers lacked Gideon's experience in coping with the detours. They followed blindly anyway, nodding bemusedly when Aunt Clara, Cousin Rufus, and Great-aunt Gertrude somehow wandered into the story, and looked sympathetic when Uncle Raymond was killed in the battle of Bull Run while charging a Damn Yankee cannon.

Gideon, enjoying himself despite the circumstances, smothered more than one laugh and saw even Farley grin from time to time. Maggie was more herself than usual, confronted by four men who'd taken one look at her and summed her up as an absolutely beautiful flake. So maybe, Gideon thought, the detours were a bit more elaborate and confusing than they might otherwise have been, since she was reflecting flakiness.

The police chief followed her as far as Bull Run, and then, made of sterner stuff than his fellows, rubbed his forehead and said, "But ma'am, wasn't that the Civil War?"

"Well, of course it was."

"Yea, ma'am. What's that got to do with bonds and a magician who fell into a well?"

"Nothing at all. Why did you think it did?"

"Because you said—" He stopped, visibly counted to ten or twenty, then resumed in a very steady voice. "Ma'am, you say that this man here in the Scottish outfit, he stole some bonds from a company in California. That right?"

"Yes. And—"

He held up a hand. "Please, ma'am, I want to try to understand this. The Scot, he joined the carnival in Little Rock, and four years later, your cousin the magician found one of the bonds and threatened to go to the police. That was in Iowa, ma'am?"

"Yes," Maggie answered patiently.

"Okay. There was an argument between the Scot and the magician, and the magician accidently fell into a well. The Iowa police, they ruled it accidental death. Then you joined the carnival because you didn't think your cousin's death was an accident, and you wanted to find out what had happened."

"Yes."

"You didn't know about the bonds?"

"Not then. Not until Balthazar was gored by a rhinoceros and Gideon came."

The chief rubbed his face slowly with both hands. "Um," he said somewhat helplessly between his fingers.

Gideon, who didn't like seeing his fellow man in distress, spoke up then to clarify matters, explaining how he came to arrive at the Wonderland carnival. He sort of skirted Balthazar's supposed fate, choosing instead to simplify the whole thing by being logical. Unfortunately, he had to cover several things that didn't quite fit the bill, such as Sean's bear pond. And a few other things wandered unconsciously into his retelling, until the straining expressions around him indicated that he wasn't making much more sense than Maggie had.

It was all really very involved.

The chief finally waved a hand for silence. He frowned a moment in thought, then handed the manila envelope over to one of his men. "Here, Greg, you call the California State Police and tell them we've got some bonds that might have been stolen a few years back. And you, Kevin, you call Iowa State Police and ask about that magician and the well."

The young officer said, "But Chief, I don't even know the man's name—"

Testily, his chief said, "Well, for Pete's sake, how many magicians could have fallen into wells in Iowa since spring?"

The young officer scurried for his desk and phone.

Farley, who had begun chuckling, looked at Gideon and said cheerfully, "You know, it's almost worth getting caught to listen to all this."

The fourth officer, standing behind his chief's chair, looked totally confused. "Who's Leo?" he asked plaintively.

Eventually, it was all sorted out—but it took a while. The California State Police contacted the San Francisco police, who opened up their files and explained their end of the case, then promised to send one of their men with the proper paperwork to extradite Farley and the bonds. One of the officers made coffee, and when Maggie said they hadn't eaten breakfast, he was sent out for doughnuts. The chief took two aspirin and talked to the Iowa police himself, rather floored to discover that two magicians had fallen into wells there since spring.

"Dangerous place for magicians," he mumbled.

"Like the Bermuda Triangle," Maggie offered judiciously.

"But that was ships and planes," the chief protested, then looked at the ceiling—or some heavenly spot beyond—and muttered, "She keeps pulling me in, and I don't want to go."

Farley, washing down a bite of doughnut with his coffee, said, "Maggie, will you testify at my trial?"

"I imagine I'll have to. Why?"

Looking pleased, he said, "No reason."

Gideon laughed despite himself, imagining the state a jury would be in after Maggie got through with them.

She looked up at him with a gleam of laughter in her eyes. "Well," she murmured for his ears only, "it was an accident, after all. And the bonds will get back where they belong."

Before Gideon could respond, the chief hung up the phone and said to the room at large, "None of this is our jurisdiction, and I don't know *why* we're— Well, never mind. This is what we're going to do. Mr. Hughes, the California police want your statement most of all because you identified the bonds and because you can place the Scot—I mean the perpetrator—in San Francisco at that company when they were stolen. So Greg is going to take you into one of the other rooms and get your statement, which you will then read and sign.

"I"—he gulped visibly—"will get Miss Durant's statement out here. After that, if you two can produce identification with a permanent address, you're free to go. Kevin, will you please put the Scot into a cell before he wanders out into the street? And read him the Miranda."

"What's the charge, Chief?" the young officer asked, still somewhat bewildered.

"He stole two point three million in bonds. Look it up, dammit."

"Doesn't anybody want my confession?" Farley asked in an aggrieved tone, getting into the spirit of things.

"You're going to be here awhile," the chief snapped. "We'll get it later."

Farley went meekly off toward the cells, his coffee in one hand and a doughnut in the other, one arm being rather gingerly held by young Kevin—who seemed as puzzled by the kilt as anything else.

Gideon obediently followed Officer Greg into a small room in the back, and the last thing he heard before the door was closed was a piteous request from the beleaguered chief as he addressed Maggie.

"All right, Miss Durant—and can we *please* keep Bull Run out of it this time?"

The taking of Gideon's statement turned out to be a long process. Officer Greg was a painstaking man who wanted every *i* dotted and every *t* crossed, and since the sequence of events was confusing to begin with, it took some time to straighten everything out. By the time Gideon read and signed his statement and emerged from the small room, a glance at his watch showed him he'd been in there nearly two hours.

Only the chief was out in front, sitting at a desk and staring at a cassette tape lying in the middle of the blotter.

"Where's Maggie, Chief?" Gideon asked as he approached the desk.

"You know," the chief said absently, "I've met just two truly unique people in my life. The first was a friend of my grandfather's. He was something. Charm spilling out over his ears, and he could talk the hind leg off a donkey. Never said much about himself, though. I didn't know till after he died that he was a war hero. At his funeral there were people from six states, four foreign countries—and the President."

After a moment Gideon said, thinking that he knew what the answer would be, "Who's the other person?"

"Her. Never met anybody like her. She's . . . sort of fascinating, isn't she?"

"She is that," Gideon said.

The chief's abstracted air vanished, and he scowled at Gideon fiercely. "None of you told me you had a tape. Why the hell not? It all makes perfect sense if you listen to the tape."

"Sorry. To tell you the truth, I forgot all about it, Chief, where's Maggie?"

"Gone."

Gideon stared at him. "Gone? Gone where?"

The chief sighed. "Colonel Sanders showed up and said he was taking her home. To tell you the truth I couldn't think of a damned reason why I should try to stop him. She left her address with us. Oh, and"—He reached into his shirt pocket and produced a folded note—"this for you."

The note was quite simple, and unsigned. In her curiously elegant script Maggie had written: *I think you should bring Leo along, don't you?*

*"Well, now that we have seen each other,"
said the Unicorn, "if you'll believe in me,
I'll believe in you. Is that a bargain?"*

Nine

Two days later, Gideon pulled his rental car into a curving driveway before a large house in an elegant old section of Richmond, Virginia. The house was imposing, to say the least, built of weathered gray stone that looked as if it might date from colonial days and sitting in the midst of perfectly manicured acreage that sloped back, eventually, to the James River.

"Wooo," Leo commented in an awed tone.

"I'll say," Gideon responded.

They stood there at the bottom of the flagged steps for a moment, the man and the cat, both just looking, and then Gideon led the way up to the massive front door and plied the gleaming brass knocker firmly.

The door opened almost immediately, revealing a severe-looking elderly man dressed in the formal and Old World attire of a butler. He didn't look surprised. He didn't look as if he'd ever been surprised by anything at all. "Good evening, Mr. Hughes," he said politely with a slight half-bow.

"Miss Durant is expecting you. Come in, please."
He stepped back, opening the door wider, and
didn't even blink when the large and rather
unusual-looking cat came in as well.

Gideon had changed quite a bit during the last
week. So much so that his strongest emotion as
he stood in the refined foyer was sheer amusement. The gleaming chandelier above his head,
the polished floor, curving staircase, huge paint-
ings of people dressed in silk, satins, and stiff
lace—all of it spoke of a family with a line so far
back it had helped to repel redcoats as well as
Damn Yankees.

No wonder Maggie had so many colorful stories
to tell, he thought wryly. Her family had probably
landed here when there was nothing more than
wilderness and savages.

"What kept you?"

He looked up, watching as she came down the
curving staircase toward him. As an entrance, it
was rather magnificent. The chameleon was wearing exquisite and dignified colors now. Her silvery
hair wound about her head in a regal coronet,
diamonds graced her throat and ears, a green silk
dress wrapped her slender body in alluring yet
sophisticated style, and matching pumps added
both height and poise to her petite form.

She fit into this setting with absolute perfec-
tion, and Gideon thought that any woman who
could belong both here and in a ragtag carnival
in the middle of a Kansas field could indeed make
herself at home wherever she chose.

In the same chiding tone she had used, he said,
"I had to go back to the camp for Leo, you know.
And naturally everybody wanted to know what
was going on, so I had to explain. One thing led to

another. In your world, it usually does. I told them we'd stop by to visit on our way to San Francisco."

"Oh, good. Gideon, this is Luther. Luther, will you see to Gideon's luggage, please?"

"Yes, Miss Maggie," the butler said, bowing slightly in acknowledgment to Gideon. "And shall I take the cat into the kitchen?"

"Yes, you shall. Hello, Leo."

"Wooo."

"Go with Luther, now, and mind your manners. They'll feed you in the kitchen." She watched the cat obediently follow the butler from the room, then took Gideon's arm companionably and guided him into a very gracious living room. "Since you've been in transit," she said, "I couldn't very well send you flowers, but the menu for tonight is very romantic, and we can go to the theater of your choice afterward."

"My preferred methods of courtship?" he asked politely, remembering what he had told her.

"Well, I thought it was only fair. Since you temporarily abandoned your job and preferred lifestyle —and with such good grace—the least I can do is to show you a little gracious living in return."

Gideon pulled her into his arms in front of a massive fireplace, above which hung a large portrait of a dark young man with laughing dark eyes dressed in the fashion of the 1890s. Ignoring the onlooker, Gideon kissed her thoroughly. "Hello," he murmured when he could.

"Hello," she answered blissfully. "Uncle Cyrus is alerting the family."

"Why didn't I get to meet him in Kansas?" Gideon demanded, detouring willingly. "Just because you wanted me to chase you halfway across the country so you could flaunt all this elegance in my face?"

"No, because he was in a hurry. He said something was starting up in Florida and he had to check on progress. He sent me home in the jet. But now he's busy disrupting airline schedules so everyone can get here quickly."

Gideon didn't even blink. "Is your mother here?"

"No, she spends most of her time in New York whenever I take a summer—um—job. She has a business there. Cosmetics. Elise Durant?"

That did surprise him. "Good Lord, she's one of the top three names in cosmetics."

"That's Mother."

"And your father was . . . ?"

"A college professor."

After a moment of considering the information, Gideon found a comfortable chair, sat down, and pulled Maggie into his lap. "I have to hear more about your family if I'm going to be facing them soon," he decided. "Do we have time before dinner to go over a few particulars?"

"Of course. What do you want to know?"

"Let's stick with immediate family for the time being. I gather you have no bothers or sisters?"

"No. How about you? I don't know very much about your family."

Gideon grinned at her. "My family is simple. Two parents, who are going to adore you once they recover from the shock, and a younger sister who falls in love once a month. I have a few aunts, uncles, and cousins scattered about, but the family isn't an especially close one."

"That's a shame," Maggie said, then added thoughtfully, "maybe we should do something about changing that."

"Maybe we should. In fact, Mom says the same, so you two can put your heads together and work on it. Now, how about grandparents?"

"Daddy's parents are still alive. Very much so. They live on a ranch in Montana. And their parents live in Charleston, so I have great-grandparents. After that, it gets a little fuzzy, and I'm not sure."

"I'm not surprised." Gideon thought about it. "Who's side of the family does this house belong to?" he asked curiously.

"Daddy's. It's sort of complicated. This is what I suppose you'd call the family seat. Uncle Cyrus says he kept it because it had so much room, and everybody could visit. If it belongs to any one person, I suppose it's he, but I don't really know. By the time Daddy got married, Uncle Cyrus and Aunt Julia were traveling a lot, so we stayed here. This is where I grew up."

"Are you going to mind living in San Francisco?"

"Of course not."

"Are you sure, honey? If all your roots are here—"

She leaned over and kissed him. "My roots are anywhere I plant them, you know that. Besides, some of my ancestors probably ran around with water buckets back when San Francisco was burning down once a week."

Gideon thought about that, then said, "Do you have a family tree down on paper?"

"If one exists, I've never seen it. I know most of the stories going all the way back to the Revolution, but the connections between people are a little vague. I think Uncle Cyrus wants it that way."

"Why?"

With a gleam of amusement in her eyes Maggie said, "that's him above the fireplace."

Gideon took another look at the painting, at the handsome, dark young man with laughing eyes. "Isn't that the style of the eighteen nineties he's wearing?"

"Uh-huh."

"But that would mean he was . . ."

"Yes. Interesting, isn't it? For all I know, he might be my great-great-grandfather."

Gideon stopped trying to do arithmetic in his head; he decided he didn't want to find a total. In a firm voice he said, "If there's one thing you've taught me, sweetheart, it's that there should always be room for possibilities."

Since Gideon was feeling a bit travel-worn and wanted to shower and change before dinner, Maggie showed him to the room where his bags had been unpacked and then left him to it, saying she had to make certain all was going well in the kitchen.

He knew at a glance that the room was hers. This was Maggie from the heavily laden shelves holding books on every conceivable subject from fiction to textbooks to the beautiful old rolltop desk in the sitting area that concealed a very modern computer. The huge, four-poster bed certainly looked more than satisfactory, and the bathroom had been modernized with comfort in mind.

He showered and dressed in more formal clothing to match Maggie's elegance, thinking for perhaps the thousandth time how much he was going to enjoy being married to her. He'd never be bored, that was for sure.

Like this, for instance. This house, this side of her. She had very deliberately given herself a head start out of Kansas, wanting to change her colors so that he could see her in a setting totally opposite to the one he'd known her in. He was glad she had, because he was thoroughly enjoying the contrast.

But it didn't really matter. Her varied colors no longer shook him off balance; he saw and understood all the shades of her, appreciating the parts, because he could see the whole.

It was an enchanting whole.

Smiling to himself, Gideon left the bedroom and went downstairs, encountering his love in the foyer where she was looking at a package that had just been delivered.

"Good, it's here," he said, joining her.

"What is it?"

"Let's go into the living room, and you'll find out when you open it."

"The last time you brought me a present," she said as they went into the other room, "it was a box of clown noses."

Sitting down beside her on the couch, he laughed. "Not this time. Go ahead, open it."

She did, removing the paper and lifting the lid of the box. Inside, cushioned carefully in tissue paper, was a very old and delicate hand mirror. Despite its obvious age, the mirror had been polished to a perfect finish with no distortions, as bright as a diamond.

"Gideon, it's beautiful," she murmured.

He lifted the mirror from the box and held it up, then slowly turned it so that she could see the other side. "Something else you taught me," he said softly. "What you find on the back side of a mirror depends on how you reached it."

What he had found was an enchanted place

hand-painted in pastel colors, the brushstrokes so airy and delicate that the scene seemed dream-like. There were unicorns and dragons, elves and rainbows, lions and lambs.

Maggie stared at it for a long moment, then turned and looked up at him, her eyes lit from inside, from the very bottom, as if a star burned there eternally. "It used to hurt when I felt too much," she whispered, "and I had to turn away, because I was afraid it would disappear if I stared at it. But I don't have to look away from us, do I?"

"No, you don't have to look away," he murmured, laying the mirror aside and gathering her into his arms. "We're forever. I love you, Maggie."

"I love you, too, darling . . . so very much."

Epilogue

He stood at the balcony door of the hotel room, gazing down on the white strip of sand that was Miami Beach, a very old man with wise dark eyes whose elegant hands were folded over a gold-headed cane.

There was a rare furrow between his snowy brows, an unusual sign of disturbance, and the lovely woman watching him from a nearby chair duly took note.

"Trouble?" she asked quietly.

His voice, rich, low, curiously powerful, was more grave than usual. "I think so. It's a dangerous thing he's into."

"You'll be there," she said.

"Yes. Yes, I will." Somber, he turned to look at her. "But, this time I don't hold all the cards."

THE EDITOR'S CORNER

This summer Bantam has not only provided you with a mouth-watering lineup of LOVESWEPTs, but with some excellent women's fiction as well. We wanted to alert you to several terrific books which are available right now from your bookseller.

A few years ago we published a unique, sophisticated love story in the LOVESWEPT line called **AZURE DAYS, QUICKSILVER NIGHTS** by talented author Carole Nelson Douglas. Carole has an incredible imagination, and her idea for her next project just knocked our socks off. Set in Las Vegas, **CRYSTAL DAYS**—a June release—and **CRYSTAL NIGHTS**—a July release—are delightfully entertaining books. Each features two love stories and the crazy character Midnight Louie, who can't be described in mere words. Don't miss these two summer treats.

Speaking of treats, Nora Roberts's long-awaited next book, **PUBLIC SECRETS,** is on the stands! Nora's strengths as a writer couldn't be showcased better than in this riveting novel of romantic suspense. **PUBLIC SECRETS** is summer reading at its very best!

Now, on to the LOVESWEPTs we have in store for you! Suzanne Forster writes with powerful style about characters who are larger than life. In **THE DEVIL AND MS. MOODY,** LOVESWEPT #414, you'll meet two such characters. Edwina Moody, hot on the trail of a missing heir to a fortune, finds her destiny in the arms of an irresistible rebel named Diablo. Edwina is more than out of her element among a bunch of rough-and-tumble bikers, yet Diablo makes her feel as if she's finally found home. On his own mission, Diablo sees a chance to further both their causes, and he convinces Edwina to make a bargain with the devil himself. You'll soon discover—along with Edwina—that Diablo is somewhat a sheep in wolf's clothing, as he surrenders his heart to the woman who longs to possess him. Much of the impact of this wonderful love story is conveyed through Suzanne's writing. I guarantee you'll want to savor every word!

This month several of our characters find themselves in some pretty desperate situations. In **RELENTLESS,** LOVESWEPT #415 by Patt Bucheister, heroine Dionne Hart takes over the helm of a great business empire—and comes face-to-face once again with the man she'd loved fifteen years

(continued)

before. Nick Lyon remembers the blushing teenager with the stormy eyes, and is captivated by the elegant woman she's become. He's relentless in his pursuit of Dionne, but she can't bring herself to share her secrets with a man she had loved but never trusted, a writer who couldn't do his job and respect her privacy too. But Nick won't take no for an answer and continues to knock down the walls of her resistance until all she can do is give in to her desire. Patt will have you rooting loudly for these two people and for their happiness. If only men like Nick could be cloned!

Talk about a desperate situation! Terry Lawrence certainly puts Cally Baldwin in one in **WANTED: THE PERFECT MAN**, LOVESWEPT #416. What would you do if you'd just dumped the latest in a long line of losers and had made a vow to swear off men—then met a man your heart told you was definitely *the one*! Cally does the logical thing, she decides to be "just friends" with Steve Rousseau. But Cally isn't fooling anyone with her ploy—and Steve knows her sizzling good-night kisses are his proof. He takes his time in wooing her, cultivating her trust and faith in him. Much to his dismay, however, he realizes Cally has more than just a few broken relationships in her past to overcome before he can make her believe in forever. And just when she thinks she's lost him, Cally learns Steve really is her perfect man. All you readers who've yet to find someone who fits your personal wanted poster's description will take heart after reading this lively romance. And those of you who have the perfect man will probably think of a few more qualities to add to his list.

If you've been following the exploits of the group of college friends Tami Hoag introduced in her *Rainbow Chasers* series, you're no doubt awaiting Jayne Jordan's love story. in **REILLY'S RETURN**, LOVESWEPT #417, Jayne finds the answer her heart and soul have been seeking. Since Jayne is quite a special lady, no ordinary man could dream of winning her. It takes the likes of Pat Reilly, the Australian movie star the press has dubbed the Hunk from Down Under, to disturb Jayne's inner peace. As much as she'd like to deny it, all the signs point to the fact that Reilly is her destiny—but that doesn't make the journey into forever with him any less tempestuous. Tami has an innate ability to mix humor with tender sensuality, creating the kind of story you tell us you love so much—one that can make you laugh and

(continued)

make you cry. Don't pass up the opportunity to experience a truly memorable love story in **REILLY'S RETURN**.

At last Joan Elliott Pickart has answered your requests and written Dr. Preston Harper's story! Joan has received more mail about Preston Harper over the years than about any other character, so she wanted to take extra care to give him a special lady love and story all his own. With **PRESTON HARPER, M.D.**, LOVESWEPT #418, Joan fulfills every expectation. As a pediatrician, Preston's love for children is his life's calling, but he longs to be a real dad. The problem is, he doesn't see himself in the role of husband! When Dinah Bradshaw walks into his office with the child who's made her an instant mom, Preston's well-ordered plans suddenly fall flat. But Dinah doesn't want marriage any more than Preston had—she's got a law career to get off the ground. Can you guess what happens to these two careful people when love works its magic on them?

Next in her *SwanSea Place* series is Fayrene Preston's **THE PROMISE**, LOVESWEPT #419. In this powerful story of an impossible love Fayrene keeps you on the edge of your seat, breathless with anticipation as Conall Deverell honors a family promise to Sharon Graham—a promise to make her pregnant! Sharon vows she wants nothing else from the formidable man who'd broken her heart ten years before by claiming that the child she'd carried wasn't his. But neither can control the passion that flares between them as Sharon accepts Conall's challenge to make him want her, make his blood boil. You've come to expect the ultimate in a romance from Fayrene, and she doesn't disappoint with **THE PROMISE!**

Best wishes from the entire LOVESWEPT staff,
Sincerely,

Susann Brailey

Susann Brailey
Editor
LOVESWEPT
Bantam Books
666 Fifth Avenue
New York, NY 10103

FAN OF THE MONTH

Mary Gregg

Reading has always been a part of my life. I come from a long line of readers who consider books treasured friends. I cannot imagine a life without books—how dull and bland it would be.

LOVESWEPTs are *the best* contemporary romances due to one lady, Carolyn Nichols. From the beginning Carolyn promised quality not quantity, and she has kept her promise over the years.

Some of my favorite authors are: Sandra Brown—she must use her husband as a hero model; Kay Hooper, who I can always depend on for her wonderful sense of humor; Iris Johansen; Helen Mittermeyer; Linda Cajio; Billie Green; Joan Elliott Pickart; and Fayrene Preston, who reminds me a little of Shirley Temple.

At the end of the day I can curl up with a LOVESWEPT and transport myself back to the days of my childhood, when Prince Charming and Cinderella were my friends. After all, romance stories are modern fairy tales for grown-ups, in which the characters live happily ever after.

THE DELANEY DYNASTY

THE SHAMROCK TRINITY

☐	21975	RAFE, THE MAVERICK *by Kay Hooper*	$2.95
☐	21976	YORK, THE RENEGADE *by Iris Johansen*	$2.95
☐	21977	BURKE, THE KINGPIN *by Fayrene Preston*	$2.95

THE DELANEYS OF KILLAROO

☐	21872	ADELAIDE, THE ENCHANTRESS *by Kay Hooper*	$2.75
☐	21873	MATILDA, THE ADVENTURESS *by Iris Johansen*	$2.75
☐	21874	SYDNEY, THE TEMPTRESS *by Fayrene Preston*	$2.75

THE DELANEYS: *The Untamed Years*

☐	21899	GOLDEN FLAMES *by Kay Hooper*	$3.50
☐	21898	WILD SILVER *by Iris Johansen*	$3.50
☐	21897	COPPER FIRE *by Fayrene Preston*	$3.50

THE DELANEYS II

☐	21978	SATIN ICE *by Iris Johansen*	$3.50
☐	21979	SILKEN THUNDER *by Fayrene Preston*	$3.50
☐	21980	VELVET LIGHTNING *by Kay Hooper*	$3.50